I0727503

SCANDAL
THE DEATH OF A LEGACY
A CONTEMPORARY ROMANCE
BY
JOHNNY RAY

**SCANDAL
THE DEATH OF A
LEGACY
Johnny Ray
Copyright © 2012
SIR JOHN PUBLISHING
ISBN #978-1-940949-19-2**

**ALL RIGHTS ARE HEREBY RESERVED
BY JOHNNY RAY**

This literary work may not be reproduced or transmitted in any form, or by any means, including, but not limited to electronic, or photographic reproduction, in whole, or in part, without the express written permission of Johnny Ray.

All characters and events in this novel are the fictitious creation of Johnny Ray. Any resemblance to any actual persons living or dead is strictly coincidental.

JOHNNY RAY

Johnny Ray is an award winning novelist who won the Royal Palm literary award for best thriller and is quickly making a name for himself as the master of the romantic thriller. He loves social interaction with his readers and can be found on

Twitter **www.twitter.com/sirjohn_writer**

Facebook **www.facebook.com/authorjohnnyray**.

He can also be reached by e-mailing at **sirjohnnyray@gmail.com**,

Or you can just follow him on his blog at

www.sirjohn.us

For updates and future releases.

Johnny Ray's other novels include:

DRONES
Published by Sir John Publishing in 2013

A WAR HERO RETURNS
Published by Sir John Publishing in 2013

JOHN RAIN – THE HAWAIIAN AFFAIR
Published by AMAZON DIGITAL in 2013

MODELS AND LOVERS
Published by Sir John Publishing in 2012

HER HONOR'S BODYGUARD
Published by Sir John Publishing in 2012

FOR LOVE AND VENGEANCE
Published by Sir John Publishing in 2012

THE SALSA CONNECTION
Published by Sir John Publishing in 2012

THE JOURNEY TO WHITESTONE
Published by Sir John Publishing in 2012

STALKING LOVE
Published by Sir John Publishing in 2012

**SCANDAL
THE DEATH OF A LEGACY
BY
JOHNNY RAY**

Chapter 1

As a tingling sensation ravaged Kristina Sutherland's body, she nervously waited for the colors to change on the test strip. Damn, she couldn't be pregnant. How? She hadn't been with a guy for months now, but still, she had never missed her period before. While a spinning numbness clouded her thoughts she studied the blue strip which indicated a positive response.

While she needed help, she knew that all she would ever receive was criticism. Yes, she loved to party, but she wasn't stupid. This couldn't be happening to her. Facing her mother would be the hardest part, since she could only imagine the headlines as Barbara Sutherland, one of the top socialites in New York City had to explain how her daughter got knocked up.

Kristina hid the test kit in a drawer, since she knew that her father, Lawson Sutherland, would be home soon. She didn't want him to know. While her mother would go berserk, her father would . . . . She squeezed her eyes shut for a moment before she shuffled toward her mother's activity room where Kristina had last seen her painting. As the perspiration coating her body turned to a bitter chill, she shut the door on the way in.

Barbara turned and lowered her paint brush as she studied her daughter, who appeared to be barely able to walk, much less stand. "What is it?"

"You're not going to like this." Kristina struggled

to find a seat as her legs failed her and her mother rushed to her aid.

"Here." Barbara tossed papers and small boxes out of the seat and onto the floor. "Kristina, you look sick."

"I feel like I'm going to pass out." Kristina realized that she might lose her lunch at any moment.

Her mother knelt beside her and squeezed her hand. "You feel sweaty. What's going on with you?"

Kristina cried as she lowered her head. Each loud expression of sorrow released one wave of embarrassment after another. "Mother . . . I'm pregnant."

"Pregnant! What? Are you sure?"

"I know. I just took a test. I missed my period, and I've never ever missed one." Kristina felt her mother pull her head into her bosom. Good, she needed support and not criticism. However, she knew that it would come soon enough. The patience of her mother shocked her, since she had never reacted like this with her before. It wasn't her temperament. "I'm sorry, mother."

"I'm so sorry, but don't worry, I'll take care of you, baby. I think I know what you're going through. I'm here for you."

Kristina raised her head to face her mother. "Please, don't tell Dad."

"He'll have to know soon enough."

"I know, but I don't know who the father is, and I know he'll want to know."

"I see. It shouldn't be too hard to figure how which guy did this to you."

"Mother, you don't understand. I haven't had sex

with anyone in a long time."

"Well apparently you have."

"That's why I'm upset. I don't remember anyone, and it has been at least four months ago since I was with anyone."

Her mother offered a smile. "Then perhaps the test was wrong, and we need to have you looked at by our doctor."

"Yes, I want to see someone good, but I don't think there's any doubt. I need to know what happened to me, and I only have one possible explanation."

"Which is?"

"I'm thinking someone may have taken advantage of me when I passed out from drinking too much one night."

"Which night?" Her mother's mouth opened wide. "This sounds like rape. Are you sure?"

"No, I'm not, but I don't have any other explanations that make sense." Kristina forced her attention to the night aboard the company yacht. She remembered the heavy drinking and the partying that occurred later, but nothing else until she woke late the next day. "Mom, I really need to do some thinking before I say anything."

"I think you're hiding something." Her mother frowned. "You know you can tell me."

In a way she knew she needed her mother's help, but she also knew how she might explode, accusing others with no proof. She had to think about it when she was alone and could concentrate better. Perhaps she needed to ask some questions of others who were onboard before she said anything and maybe even find someone who could do an investigation for her—

discretely.

As Kristina mind raced from one thought to another, her mother regained her normal mannerisms of arrogance and pride she had been breed with—something Kristina had fought against every day. She didn't want to become like her mother. Her father's wealth provided her with all of the physical luxury they could ever want, but had also saddled them with a need to protect their image from those intending to ruin it in any kind of scandal. Such was the life of the high society elite in New York City.

"I can tell you're not mentally able to handle this right now. I think I have no choice but to help you."

"Mom, you mean control me, but don't worry since I don't plan to let the world know what happened until I have more answers." Kristina rubbed her eyes. "I need to be alone for a while and think."

"I do hope you have some smarts about you, but we do need to get to the bottom of this as fast as we can."

"For now, I need to lie down and rest. While I know I need to eat something, I simply want to be left alone for a while." Before her mother could respond, Kristina walked out of the room and rushed to her own. While she had to concentrate on what she needed to do, she also could really use a best friend right now; someone who really cared about her. Unfortunately, all of the people she had around her insisted on partying all of the time. They would find this hilarious, and their ridicule was definitely not what she needed now.

Her iPhone rang as she entered her room. "Hello." She waited. "Hello." She repeated as she glanced at the blank caller id. "I don't know who you are, but this call can be traced." The phone connection died. While she needed to call the phone company to see what they could do, she simply wanted to rest for a while. At twenty-five she should be on her own, but for now she felt glad to have her parents around. She walked to her bed as she unclasped her long blonde hair.

Shawn Davis enjoyed escaping to the small café in the basement of the building where several executives of the corporation he worked for lived. No one here knew his grandfather owned the building, or even cared how his dear old grandfather had thrown him and his mother to the street many years ago. Only after his mother's death did his grandfather come to his rescue, and even then the only job Shawn had been offered was that of a guard which he could only keep by hiding their relationship.

Shawn's grandfather, Brent Lyons, owned most of the stock in the software company bearing his name. While Lyons International had built a name designing security systems for major corporations around the world, their real money came from another source that fell into their laps several years ago—video games.

Shawn, however, felt proud of the way he had handled his duties, and how he had been elevated to the chief security officer for the corporation. The two competing company ventures gave him much to keep him busy. Many people around the world would love to be able to break into their files to gain codes, or even worst, kidnap one of the officers or programmers responsible for protecting the data bases of corporations they represented. The other problem was the celebrity status of those designing games.

While he had been studying programming, knowing it would come in handle one day, his skill was in providing bodyguard services to those in the company. He laughed as he thought how different his job was in comparison to how the general public perceived it.

Much of what he performed was boring, and the hours were long and often unappreciated. Still, it allowed him an excuse to pursue his favorite sport or recreation of martial arts. He even considered opening his own martial arts studio one day. While not massive in size, he knew how to handle himself, and constantly worked out when he was not on duty.

The small café only had about ten chairs, and many people didn't know it existed. Half of the tables tonight were occupied with weary men who needed a quick meal before returning to work, much like him. He did hope to finish in a few hours in order to make it to the gym before they closed.

As he watched one girl walk in, dressed in a full length overcoat pulled high upon her neck, he knew the kind—rich, arrogant, and generally a royal pain in the butt. While she looked completely out of place here, he studied her movements as she approached the counter. She didn't glance around, indicating she had been here before as she ordered without looking at the marquee above.

When she turned, their eyes met. It took a second before he recognized Kristina. Her father also worked for the corporation his grandfather owned, and in fact he also occupied a seat on the board of directors. After her glare locked in this frozen moment in time slowly thawed, a smile soon inched out of one corner of her mouth as she moved closer to him to ask, "How are you?"

"I'm fine, thanks. I'm just grabbing a bite to eat. I didn't know many people knew about this place."

"It's not on my top places to eat, but I thought no one would recognize me here." She nervously glanced around.

He watched her eventually glance at his food. "Well, at least it's fast." Shawn studied the various empty tables and knew that she had many available, but he decided to be polite. "Would you like to join me?"

He watched the indecisiveness as she twitched to one side before answering. "I guess so, but I really was looking for a place to be alone for a while to do some thinking."

"Don't worry since I can only stay for a few more minutes. I need to get back to work"

"Are you working this late?" She acted surprised but polite as she joined him.

Shawn allowed a small laugh to escape. "My work seems to never end, but all is quiet so far tonight."

"I think I've seen you around often when we travel. You do know who I am."

"Yes, I do, it's my job to know everyone connected to Lyon International." Shawn considered extending his hand to introduce himself but stopped.

Kristina laughed, but she failed to hide a pain she couldn't erase. "Knowing everyone in this company has to be a major task."

"Like I said, it's my job to keep everyone safe."

Kristina's face turned serious for a minute. "I'm not sure if you can help me, but can I ask you something, strictly between you and me?"

This was not the first time he had received special requests. He had often been used to find information on others, which he assumed she would be asking. "I should be able to, I think. Why? What is it you want to ask me?"

"I've a situation where I might need to hire a private detective, and I've never done this before. Off the record, I was wondering if you could recommend someone."

"I know many people, but first I need to know more about what you're after, since they all have different areas of expertise. And perhaps it might be something I can handle for you quietly, since it's my job to handle anything which might affect the company or its employees. Knowing who your father is, I'm sure that coverage would extend to including you."

Kristina glanced around the café for the first time. "In this case, I don't need anyone from the company hearing about this. This is why I think I need someone independent."

Shawn listened, but knew he had to know more, and to do so, he had to gain her confidence. "As you may or may not know, discretion is what I'm hired to do."

"I'll have to think about it, but there's one thing you can help me with, and this is something else no one needs to know about. Can you promise me you'll do this for me?"

"What is it you want me to do?" Shawn had learned to never make an open promise without knowing all of the details.

"I know you're good at getting people in and out of places without being seen. I've seen you help my dad do this before."

"Yes, one of the best ways to protect someone is to find an easy way to enter and exit a building. " Shawn noticed a small quiver coming from her body. Something was up.

"I may need to see a special doctor."

Alarms went off. If he read this correctly, he had a girl in trouble who could also get him in trouble if he didn't handle it right. "Do you think you're pregnant?"

Kristina ducked her head and glanced over her shoulder. "Please, not so loud." She raised her head as her eyes focused on him. "Please forget what I said. I need to handle this on my own and not let my father know."

"Please, calm down. I'm here to help. Why don't you visit your family doctor?"

"My regular doctor is good friends with my father."

Now he understood. "An appointment with another doctor shouldn't be too hard."

"Can you help me see one with no questions asked, and where I'll not be seen leaving or entering the building?"

"We can have one come visit you at your home if you wish."

"No, it has to be outside somewhere. I don't even want my mother involved. There has to be a place that handles sensitive cases like mine and is still reputable. I don't want to go to a butcher or some low class place."

"I'll see what I can find for you." He had to do

some major checking on this later.

"Thanks. I'll call tomorrow morning to ask for you to take me shopping. That will be our cover."

Shawn needed to think. If this went bad, he could be fired. "What about the father? Shouldn't he be involved in this?"

He watched her unfocused eyes fill with water. "I don't know who it is. This is why I want to hire a private detective."

"Now . . . I see. This I can help you with, but I'll need a lot of information from you."

Shawn watched her bite her lip. "It's not like you think. I don't remember having sex with anyone for months. I think I may have been raped." She closed her eyes.

Shawn knew she might be having major issues with her nerves, so he decided to move slowly. "That's a big accusation. Do you have any one in particular you think might have done this?" While he waited for an answer, he needed to get her out of the small café where someone who knew her might venture in.

"No, absolutely none. I have one guy I see occasionally, but I don't think he would do this."

"Okay, we'll talk more tomorrow. Can I help you back to your place?"

"Yes, I think it would be good for you to help me. Well . . . at least to my elevator. I can make it from there."

Chapter 2

Shawn woke as the sun's early morning glare flooded his flat. The sloppy kisses coming from Lucy, his large black retriever, insured that he would not be late for his morning run. With Central Park less than ten blocks away, he had designed a course which managed to give him a five mile run before he returned.

He felt lucky finding this place, which he had converted a year ago into his living quarters. His grandfather owned this building which had unused space above the shops below. While this space must have functioned as an office of some kind earlier, it provided the space he needed to exercise and practice his martial arts. His place covered the corner of the building and only had the one large room and one small bathroom.

At twenty-seven he felt like he had already settled into his ways of a bachelor for life. The few women in his past, with the solo exception of his mother, had only caused him problems. His mother had done the best she could for him and had kept him off of the street. A picture of her hanging on the wall next to his bed received the ritual kiss of finger to photo as he rose.

After walking into the kitchen area, Shawn fed Lucy before he turned on his favorite music that he had composed from various movies he had enjoyed watching. He went from one exercise to the next like a seasoned dancer with each movement so well rehearsed that he could have done them in his sleep. The words of his mother echoed in his head, as he remembered her telling him the difference between a successful man and a failure was the ability to take advantage of an opportunity. Since this required preparation, she had forced him to exercise every morning.

When he reached for the leash, Lucy bounded after him as he opened his door. From the outside, no one would ever know a person actually lived in the building. Since he did no entertaining, this was perfect for him. He liked being out of sight, and in many cases out of mind. No one had ever cared about him except his mother, and she had died five years ago. It was only then that his grandfather ever paid him any attention, but why now? He might not ever know the truth, but his grandfather had thankfully given him a job and a place to live.

As the city came to life in the early morning dawn, he saw many of the same runners and business men making their normal early appearances. The night people had already left the park. While some people felt apprehensive running alone, he never felt safer, since another legacy his mother had forced upon him was his martial art training.

In the solitude of his run along the street, his thoughts turned to the girl he had talked to the night before. He had to be careful. While he felt sorry for her, and wanted to help her, he knew who he owed allegiance to. There had to be much more to her story. In a weakened state she had appeared much softer and more vulnerable than she normally did, but he had worked with many rich women and their daughters, who had such stuffy pretentiousness about them on many occasions before.

Shawn continued his jog until he reached a small cafe on a corner that he always stopped at to eat a bagel with crème cheese, which was his one vice in the morning. The large black coffee had also become a custom of his as he walked back to his building. After he entered a side door to his apartment, and climbed the steps to finish his workout, he needed to hurry and take a quick shower before dressing for his job. He hated the look, but it was something they had forced upon him.

As Lucy walked to her bed near the darkest corner, Shawn wished he could have a back yard for her to play, but he didn't anticipate that happening for a long time. "Stay out of trouble, Lucy. I don't need another girl getting me in trouble right now." Shawn shook his head, knowing he had to use discretion in what he did today.

Kristina had slept little, if any, during the night, with every late night party she had recently attended churning in her mind. Working on solutions to her problems drove her close to insane. While she thought she knew half of the people living in the city, no one person rose through the ranks to become her champion or trusted confident when she needed one.

Her mother had remained quiet all night after her father had walked through the front door of their condo. While she hoped her mother was smart enough to not involve him at this point, she knew that as soon as her father left for his office that she would have many more questions for her when she walked out of her bedroom.

Kristina didn't plan to allow her mother much of an opportunity to do so as she swung her door open and marched out. Barbara quickly yelled at her as expected. "Where are you going?"

"Out. I need some answers."

"Surely you're not planning on doing something stupid!"

Kristina forced a special smile that she knew her mother hated. "I'm not going to do anything to embarrass you. As you suggested, I want a professional to give me another test to determine if I'm really pregnant."

"Who are you going to see?"

"I'm going somewhere they don't ask a lot of questions."

"I think this is something we need to talk about, don't you? Don't you think the news media will have a heyday with photos of you going to a doctor for such tests?" Her mother straightened her back, signifying her willingness to do battle.

"I thought about this already. We made some plans to avoid the press or anyone for that fact."

"We—who?"

"I ran into the guy who is the head of security for the company last, and I asked him to help me. He's trained at helping people get in and out of places without being seen."

Kristina watched the mixed signals float across her mother's face. "I'm not going to ask how you planned this, but if he can keep his mouth shut I think he can be a big help to us. We still don't know what all we'll be facing with this."

"I received his word that he would be discrete. I'm sure this is something he knows how to handle."

"Yes, but remember who he works for—your father."

"I know, but even if dad finds out I'm sure he'll be glad I used him. I hope he never has to find out, and that this is all a mistake."

"Do you want me to go with you? I can be ready in a few minutes."

Kristina knew better. She always required hours to get ready to go anywhere. "Mother, you know the chances of being spotted would be much higher if you're with me."

"You know I can have a doctor come here."

"No, I've thought about it, and I want to do this on my own. I need some time to think also. Shawn said he would help me determine who the father might be."

"It sounds like you may have already divulged maybe more than you should."

"He knows very little. What I asked for is the name of a private detective who could work discreetly for me."

"So . . . you still don't know who the father is?"

"Not yet, but I intend to find out."

"See what you can remember, and I'll try to run interference for you for as long as I can." Her mother surprised her, since Kristina was fully expecting yelling and accusations. Perhaps her mother was still in shock.

"Mother, that's exactly what I need for now. Thanks." Before her mother asked any more questions, or changed her attitude, Kristina walked out and made the call to have Shawn available to take her shopping. Shopping . . . what a funny word for what she had to do.

Shawn glanced at the clock as the phone call came in. At least she was punctual. "Hello, this is Shawn."

A different voice from what he expected responded. "Hello, Shawn. Can you come see me a minute?" The sound of his grandfather's voice irritated him, sending verbal salt to old wounds. But still, Brent had given him a life line that he needed.

"Sure, I can be in your office in a few minutes." Being the CEO of the company, and not to mention his grandfather, he had little choice. He still wondered, however, what the old man would want him to do next.

"Good." The phone line died with no hello or good bye, just business as usual.

Shawn stood to check the outfit that he detested, but he knew his grandfather expected him to wear. While not looking specifically like a uniform, since it also incorporated a business looking suit in it, the uniform was designed to be functional. He always dressed fully armed with one shoulder mount ready at all times, and one ankle for back up. He stayed in contact with his staff by use of an earplug that he constantly wore.

Shawn checked in with the front guard on the way up. "I think our meeting will be late today, since I'm on the way to see Lyons now."

"Not a problem, all is going smooth this morning."

In addition to the guards for the headquarters building, Shawn also oversaw the guards throughout the properties owned by the company. He also had his elite group of five men, which functioned more or less as bodyguards and drivers for the executives of the company. He was never disillusioned about how much of a target these men were to any kind of terrorist group or even a competing company, be it local or international. These men had the keys to the data files of many of the top companies in the world.

A few minutes later, Brent's secretary opened the door for him to his grandfather's office. As far as she knew, Shawn was simply one of the security people. Brent had his back to him, and he was looking out over the city as Shawn walked toward his massive desk setting in a room large enough to accommodate ten or more people anywhere else in the company.

Shawn knew his grandfather made him wait on purpose. It was almost like a game Brent played, until he finally turned. "I'm glad you could make it so fast. Please . . . have a seat."

A seat? His grandfather had never asked him to make himself comfortable before. After Shawn studied his face and saw no signs of a smile, he assumed that he had lots of details to discuss and wanted to let him know that he would be in his office for a while. Brent reached for a pad to make some notes.

"You can put that away. I want to talk to you off the record." He looked over the top of his glasses, and spoke kind of down his nose toward Shawn, a posture Shawn had disliked forever.

"Okay. Is there something I'm doing wrong, grandfather?"

Brent looked around to make sure no one was close by. "I know you don't understand, but scandals are the one thing we don't need at this company. I'll admit that I made some mistakes, and I should have done more for your mother. If I could do it over again, I would."

"I see. She had a hard life."

"I hate to say it, but she brought much of it on herself. She's the one who ran off with your father, who as far as we can tell is still on the run somewhere around the world."

"The last I heard he had a band touring in Germany."

"So . . . you do still keep up with him?"

"Not really, but one day I'll face him man to man."

"I'm sure you will." Brent paused. "How is the new job working out? I'm glad to see you're doing well in your management position."

"It's fine. Thanks for the help."

"I did nothing. You earned it on your own. I personally thought you would quit after a few weeks."

"I've gained a lot of experience, which I'm sure will be helpful later."

"Shawn, what is it you want to do?"

Shawn considered letting him know about his plans, but decided not to share them for now. He would not understand how much he loved his martial arts, or how he planned to open a special school to teach bodyguards later. He wanted to provide training for the best while running a world class bodyguard service. "I'm working on some things."

Shawn heard the sound of the speaker phone activating as Brent's secretary interrupted them. "I'm sorry, sir, but I have Kristina Sutherland on the other line, and she's looking for Shawn."

Brent's eyes widened as he turned to Shawn who decided to play dumb and act like he had no idea why she was looking for him. Brent clicked on the intercom. "You can pass it back here and Shawn can take it at my desk."

This was not what he wanted, but he leaned forward to accept the ringing phone on line two. "Hello, this is Shawn."

"I've been trying to reach you this morning."

"I'm sorry. Mr. Lyons called me to his office this morning to go over a few things." Shawn knew what she was thinking, but he wasn't selling her out. "Is there a problem I can help you with?"

"I want to go shopping today over in the garment district, and my mother insists I have someone go with me. I hate to disturb your meeting however."

"No, it's not a problem at all. When do you want me to pick you up?"

"As soon as you can get here would be good."

Shawn lowered the phone. "I have someone wanting me to take her somewhere. Is there anything else we need to discuss?" He did this on purpose to allow Kristina to hear.

Brent's voice regained a business, no-nonsense tone. "No, I think that'll be all today."

Shawn raised the phone to his ear. "I'll meet you at the front entrance of your condo in a few minutes." He knew he would have to answer some questions as he returned the phone to its holder.

"We do need to talk more later about your plans." He paused, and focused his attention directly into Shawn's eyes. "How often do you usher Kristina around?"

"I think this is the first time she has asked specifically for me, but Barbara Sutherland, her mother, often does."

"Take very good care of her. I know she can be a handful, much like her mother, but Lawson, her father, is a major stockholder at the company. We go way back." Shawn studied a tense stressful vibration in his grandfather's voice he hadn't noticed earlier.

"I will. It's good to see you again, grandfather." He knew he shouldn't do that, but he couldn't resist. Okay, Brent had helped him out with the job and all, but he had earned his keep. While regaining his respect would be another thing, there would be another day.

Chapter 3

Kristina was having second thoughts. What was Shawn doing in old man Lyons office, of all places? He had promised not to tell anyone, and Lyons would be the last guy she would want to know, since he was a good friend of her father. Her hands sweated under her gloves, but she wanted them on since she knew how cold it would be outside.

From behind the glass door she watched a town car pull in front of the entrance where she waited for him. After he opened the door and said hello to the doorman who appeared to recognize him, she studied him intensely, wanting to know an immediate answer. Still, she knew that she had to get inside the car first before asking questions. "It took you long enough." Kristina watched the doorman smile out of the side of his face. She knew she could be a bitch at times, but nobody knew how much she really needed others to care about her right now.

"Sorry, I hurried as much as possible," she heard him say as she walked as fast as she could and entered the town car before she said the wrong thing.

He quickly jumped into his seat and raced off for a few blocks before he spoke. "Where do you want to go?"

"First . . . I want to know what you were doing in Mr. Lyons office."

"He called me first thing this morning and wanted to see me about some future event he's planning."

"And you want me to believe you said nothing about talking to me?"

"The truth is . . . I should have, but I didn't since I really don't have a lot to tell him, and at this point, I don't see anything he should be aware of. This should be none of his business. I told you I would keep this quiet if I can."

"So what did you tell him after I called?"

"Just that you wanted me to take you shopping. He told me to take good care of you."

"Okay, a word to the wise . . . I need you and I hope you can keep your word about keeping your mouth shut. I really don't need this shit today."

Shawn smiled, but he appeared to be biting his tongue to stay quiet. "I've been told to take care of you personally, so what can I do?"

"I've the name of a doctor out of the city, who is supposed to be discrete. Here's the name and address." She handed him a piece of paper with the information on it.

"How did you get this name?"

She hated to admit it but gave in. "I got it off the internet. I've never had to play a cloak and dagger type life before."

She watched him pull off the road for a minute. "Would you like for me to make some calls first?"

She did feel uneasy going to a perfect stranger. "Do you have contacts where I won't be seen?"

"I can make some calls. This guy you have an appointment with might be good, but please give me a minute."

"I didn't make an appointment. This place doesn't require one, and you don't have to give a name. I just want to confirm that I'm pregnant with no one else knowing for now."

"This sounds like one of those abortion clinics."

"Yes, but I've no plans on having an abortion. I'll hire a good doctor later if I decide to have one. This is one of those places where they don't ask a lot of questions, which is what I want for now."

"Are you sure you want to do this?"

"Yes . . . and I need your help to make sure I'm not spotted."

"I'll need to stop and change cars, since this town car will be exactly what we don't need. I can rent one on the way."

Kristina hadn't thought about it, but it made a lot of sense, since she assumed most of the people there would be poor, and definitely not showing up with a corporate driver. "Yes . . . and even an older car would be better. What kind of car do you own?" She felt the car slowing.

"You don't really want to know."

"Yes I do. What is it?"

"I have a mini cooper which is a few years old."

"Really?" While Kristina had never been in one, she had heard they could be a blast. She suddenly wished she had learned to drive so she could have made this trip herself, but by growing up in the city she had no need for a car, and when she did it was always provided for her.

"It would be the best way to get you in and out without being noticed, but I promise you that it's not near as comfortable as what you're used to."

"I'm not as fragile as you might think. I think I'd prefer to try going in your car."

###

Shawn pulled into the side alley before entering his parking place near the back loading dock of the building he lived in. After he located a place to park, he looked around as he opened the door for Kristina. Her eyes showed a new fear as she stepped out of the town car. "You live here?"

"No, not down here, but in the penthouse above." He loved the humor in his words, since she would never see it.

He watched her step lightly as she followed closely behind him. Since the old oil on the floor might ruin her shoes, he felt glad he had parked close to his car. After he opened the passenger door for her to enter, he held her hand as she lowered herself into the seat. When she lifted her legs to pull her feet in her dress rose high on her legs, revealing a straight shot up her dress. While he turned his head immediately, he still got a clear view at her skimpy panties. To his surprise, she smiled at him as he shut the door.

After he rounded the car, he jumped into his seat. "I really hope you appreciate this, since this could get me fired."

"I don't think so. If I handle this properly, I'll be saving my parents and the company a lot of embarrassment. You might not ever be rewarded for your efforts, but you would have accomplished what you're hired to do."

He knew that she was right, and it was the only reason he agreed to this. "Do you have a scarf or something to wear on your head? You're still well known in the city, and this car makes it easy for someone to spot you."

"I can sit back and keep my head down, if you wish."

He knew he had made a mistake. "Yes, this car is not near as safe as the company car."

As he stopped outside the garage and lowered the door to hide the town car, Kristina leaned sideways to study the building. "What's the name of the building you live in?"

"It doesn't really have one."

"It looks like a commercial warehouse of some kind."

"Yes . . . it is, but I converted the top floor to a living area which works out great for me."

"Really! I've heard of many people doing conversions in the city, but I don't think I've been in any."

"Like I said, it works for me." One thing he felt sure of—she would never see it.

He hit the gas and hurried toward the tunnel leading out of the city, thinking that the sooner he made it through, the better. For a moment he relaxed when on the other side blue skies and parting clouds greeted them. It would be a good day to have a drive outside the city. Shawn plugged in the address on his GPS.

When Kristina turned her head to study the scenery, Shawn checked her out, as if for the first time. She had many great features, including long, thick, blonde hair, which was cut in layers, flattering her face. It seemed to radiate as the light reflected the golden color.

When she turned to face straight ahead, he studied

the fear in her eyes. Instead of having friends around her to protect her, she had to depend on a bodyguard supplied by the company. He wished he really knew what was going on inside her mind.

She turned her head in his direction. "I didn't realize these cars were so fast."

Shawn checked his speed, and slowed from the eighty he was cruising. "Yes, they can fly." He glanced at the estimated time of arrival. "We should be there in about forty-five minutes."

As Kristina turned toward the passenger window, Shawn studied her again. Rich girls always confused him. They had everything, but they always complained about having nothing. On the outside they always acted tough, but inside they were so, well using the words of Kristina—fragile.

Her suit, perfectly tailored to her lean fit body, probably cost more than he made in a month. The beige color complimented her skin tone. He felt sure it had a designer name attached to it, but who the hell was he to know which one?

Suddenly Kristina turned to him with a small hiccup of a cry. "I can't believe this is happening to me."

He felt like comforting her, but he really had no experience in this. He seldom had a girl around he could call a girlfriend. "I'm sorry, and I hope everything works out for you."

The next question caught him off guard. "Are you married, or do you have a girlfriend?"

"I have neither." He thought about adding more details, but why should he?

Kristina went back to biting her lower lip, a habit

she demonstrated often when she revealed a nervous trait. "There're times like this, I wish I had a brother, or a real boyfriend who cared about me."

Shawn knew to not ask questions, but the vulnerability he witnessed, and the inner helplessness, prodded him to know more. "I would think you would have many guys who wanted to be your boyfriend."

"I have one guy in an on again, off again, relationship, but it's more of a convenience thing. We both have many functions we have to attend." She stopped to look at him. "I know what you're thinking, and I don't think it's him, but I've no way of knowing for sure."

Shawn had seen her with one guy before, and he hoped this wasn't the guy she was referring to. Jeff Jones was the president of the company. He was almost forty and perhaps fifteen years older than Kristina. While he had never married, he had a reputation at times of being a playboy, which Shawn knew was undeserved, since he had to provide bodyguard services for him on many occasions.

"I'm sure a DNA test will prove who the father is."

"Yes, I've thought about it. Because of many complications I'd love to know who it is as soon as I can. I still need to know more about how they will obtain the baby's DNA. I assume they can before I give birth, but this is one of the questions I hope to get answered today."

As if for the first time, Shawn realized what she was facing if she had no clue who had impregnated her. "I can understand your predicament. I want to help."

"Why should you care?"

"Don't get me wrong. I'm not a knight in shining armor type."

She interrupted him while he wanted to explain, but perhaps it was a good thing, and before he said something he might regret later. "I understand. This could also explode into a scandal which you're hired to prevent or at least minimize."

"Something like that." Shawn knew the ramifications, and didn't like the position it would place him in.

"It's not much, but at least it's good to know that we have a common goal. Have you thought anymore about who would be a good private detective for me?"

Shawn ran some names through his mind, and knew of several possibilities. "As I mentioned to you earlier, it would be good to get some more information on what you need a private detective for."

"I think you understand now that I don't know who the father is, and it's not because I sleep around a lot. I don't!"

"I'm not here to place blame. I'm not like that." Shawn wanted to know more, but he also knew that she had a reputation, much like Mr. Jones.

She smiled as she glanced at him out of the corner of her eye. "We only have a few minutes until we get there, so let me just say this. I only have one time that I'm suspicious of."

Now he was getting somewhere. "I know this is hard for you, but I promise to keep this as quiet as possible."

"I went on a short cruise aboard the company yacht a little over a month ago. I'm sure you might remember it."

Shawn knew the corporate yacht well, and had been on it many times. The assignments were always interesting in keeping the passengers safe from potentially being boarded, but it was mostly from them hurting themselves while overdrinking. "The yacht is used often, do you know the date? I can do some checking on it."

"I can look it up, but it was the first weekend in September."

"I think I remember it, and while I wasn't on board we did have several of my men there. I don't remember any problems being reported."

"I know this sounds farfetched, but I had some drinks the night of the cruise, and I had to sleep it off in one of the cabins. But truthfully, I don't remember drinking that much. I only remember waking the next morning with a bad headache, and being driven home. The whole night is still fuzzy."

"Why didn't you say anything earlier?"

"I didn't like being known as a drunk. The one guy I was interested in was Jeff, but he had a new girlfriend on board, which is why I don't think he did anything to me."

"I hope you don't mind me asking the obvious question."

Kristina looked sideways at him, and bit her lip again. "I think I know what you're going to ask."

"Perhaps . . . but I still need to know since I'm sure it'll come up later. Assuming you were drugged, or you passed out by drinking too much, why didn't you know you had sex the night before? Shouldn't you have noticed something . . . unusual?"

For the first time he watched her blush. "I don't

remember going downstairs, but I heard later that Jeff had helped me. I also heard he was seen with his new girlfriend dancing soon afterwards. I barely remember waking the next morning and climbing in the limo to drive back to the city."

"I hope you excuse me for asking this."

"I assume you want to know if I noticed anything different in my clothing, or my body, which would indicate I was raped." Shawn knew this was a time to remain quiet. "I woke in the same clothes I wore the night before. I smelled bad, as I must have perspired during the night with all of my clothes on. I never sleep with my clothes on, or even my underwear. Like many girls, I enjoy the freedom. I thought the slight disarrangement in my clothes came from sleeping in them."

"I see."

"And yes, I'm not a virgin. I'm twenty-five years old and I've had boyfriends before, just not anytime lately. The last time I remember was about four or five months ago with Jeff. Now, does that answer your questions?"

"I'm not sure all of them, but it provides me with something to work on. It'll take a little time to interview my guys who worked the cruise. I'll get on it tomorrow, if not tonight. " He watched her stare. "Don't worry. I'll be cautious on digging for the truth. Trust me." Shawn pointed to the GPS. "We'll be there in a few minutes."

###

Kristina studied the entrance. "Oh shit!" A line of protestors lined the street in front of the clinic; so much for the advertising about being discrete. She watched Shawn glide by the entrance.

"Perhaps we need to go somewhere else." Shawn pulled into a quick stop, while her heart continued to beat fast.

"No, I want to get this over with. There has to be a way to get by them." Kristina turned her head to look out the window.

Shawn twisted to face her. "I'll circle the block and see if there's a back entrance. Why don't you stay here and see about getting us a coke or something. It's best if I go alone first."

Kristina looked at the entrance to the quick stop." Surely you don't intend to drop me off here?"

"It's your choice. Do you want to be recognized?"

"I see your point. Please don't leave me here long." Kristina opened her own door, and lumbered toward the entrance as she heard Shawn pulling off behind her.

By the time she purchased a coke for him and a large water for herself, he drove back into the parking lot, jumped out of the car, and helped her to her seat. "We can make it past them and they have a private entrance in the back. We do need to do one thing. Stay here and I'll be back in a minute." He opened his door and rushed inside the quick stop.

Kristina had a sickening feeling in her stomach again. What was she doing out in the middle of nowhere? This was becoming a very bad idea. She needed a good doctor and the will to face the music.

Shawn soon returned with a large ski type hat. "Here, this will do."

Kristina looked at the most hideous hat she had ever seen. "You don't think I'm going to wear that, do you?"

"I guess it depends on if you want to be recognized or not. You have very beautiful hair that's easy to recognize."

She had received many compliments on her hair, and many times she had paid them no attention. But something in the way he referred to it, lingered in her mind. There was something different about Shawn. He was one of the few men who didn't hit on her. He had used the word beautiful as a given, and not as an advance. Perhaps this was in keeping with his job, but still, it felt good. She glanced at the hat.

"I promise, you'll only have it on for a minute or two."

As she slipped the hat on and smiled, his eyes focused on her face, studying her in a way she wasn't prepared for. "You're still beautiful, but I think we'll be okay." He turned on the motor and headed for the entrance. "Be sure to duck lower as we make it past the people out front."

She followed his instructions, but glanced at the signs. The first one startled her by calling her a baby killer. What baby? She didn't consider it a baby. It was simply a problem she had to take care of.

After pulling into a spot, Shawn moved quickly to her door, helped her out, and rushed her toward the back door of the clinic. She breathed easier as she walked inside where a female nurse greeted them in seconds. "How are you?"

"I got the address of your place online this morning, and I decided to come here based on how discrete you claimed to be. I didn't know you would have so many people out front."

"We're sorry about that. They showed this morning, but our attorney says he'll have them off the property soon. I hope by the time we're finished with you."

The words, "finished with you" didn't sound right. "I decided to come here to verify if I'm pregnant or not. I'm not here for an abortion yet."

"I understand. Verification is the first step in the process. We never push anyone into something they don't want. We simply provide you with options. I'll find you some forms to complete."

"I really don't want to fill out any forms."

"Our service is covered by insurance."

"Not necessary, I'm paying cash." Kristina flashed a hundred dollar bill. When the girl simply smiled but stood still, Kristina added another hundred. "I simply want verification and the answers to a few quick questions."

The girl reached over and accepted the money. "Follow me." She stopped for a second and looked at Shawn. "Is this the father?"

A sense of shock overtook her. Did the nurse think she would really make it with her bodyguard? She stopped herself, as she realized she might give herself away. "No, he's a friend giving me a ride." Her eyes locked on his. Except for his status in life, he had many characteristics she liked, and especially the way he looked at her: not staring with his eyes, but offering support in a powerful, unspoken way.

"I see. He can wait for you out here in the lobby." She pointed to a chair.

Minutes later, she was taking another test where she hoped to have the answer soon. As she waited, the nurse gave her some information on the services they offered. They made it appear so clinical—so cold.

The nurse soon walked back in. "Yes, you're pregnant. Since this guy you're with isn't the father, let me ask you some questions. Do you want the real father to know you're pregnant, or end it here without him knowing?"

"I don't know who the father is."

"Sorry, but I need to ask. Were you raped?"

"It's possible yes, but it's . . . complicated."

"Like I said, I'm sorry for having to ask you these questions." She handed her another flyer. "Sexually transmitted diseases are a problem these days. Have you been tested recently?"

"I don't think I have any kind of disease."

"If you don't know who the father is, how can you be sure?"

She felt sick and hoped she could control her sudden urge to puke. "I never thought of it before."

"We can test you here and give you the results in a few days. It'll be discreet, I promise."

She felt like she had no choice. "I don't want you to send me the report, I'll have someone come by and collect it in a week. Will that be enough time?"

"Yes, that should do. I'm going to leave you with a package of information. We're here to help you, but remember, the earlier you take care of your decision, the better."

Thoughts of having an abortion didn't seem possible. Was she really carrying a human body inside her? She blinked as she suddenly wondered—is it a boy or a girl? Oh God, she didn't need this. While her mind played havoc, the nurse stayed still. She felt lightheaded. She needed to leave for now. She had to think. She, however, cleared her head long enough to ask one more question. "I still don't know who the father is. Is it possible to get a DNA sample of the baby without hurting it?"

"Yes, the results take about two weeks to obtain, but you need to be further along than you are now."

"If I was raped, I want to know who the father is."

"Have you reported this to the police yet?"

"I don't know what to report."

"Here, let me give you one more number you might want to call." She handed her a small postcard sized brochure. "This is from a rape center which might be of help to you."

Kristina looked at the words. Rape. She had been so concentrated on taking care of her body and mind, trying to decide how this happen to her, that the thoughts of being raped had never seemed to register until now. For the first time, she felt the rage, the anger. Who was the bastard who did this? She would find out.

"Thank you for everything, but I'm not ready to make a decision yet. I'll stay in touch."

"We'll be here, and next time we won't have the people out front."

Chapter 4

Shawn pulled into the parking spot next to the town car. The guys working for him had covered perfectly without asking too many questions. He knew, however, his grandfather would ask questions later. Well, maybe not, he had lots on his plate.

Images of the people protesting the clinic invaded his thoughts again. They took their mission seriously, as he had to practically run over them to leave the clinic. Their baby killer signs proved effective, as he watched Kristina's face studying them. She would be under enormous pressure soon, and he hoped he could help her.

After he walked around to her side to open the door, she extended her hand for help in climbing out. He didn't mind; it gave him a chance to hold her hand, a soft yet warm connection he had avoided for most of his life. "I'll have you back home in a few minutes."

He watched her studying the garage before glancing upward. "You really live here?"

"Yes. I'll assure you, it's nothing like Fifth Avenue here."

"I don't really mean to be a bother, but I don't want to face my dad yet. Can I come up for a minute?"

Shawn's mind said no as he wasn't prepared for anyone to get close to him, or see how he lived. "I'm . . . not so sure visiting my loft would be a good thing."

"Why not, we need to talk. I want you to find out who did this to me."

Shawn really didn't want to do this, but he knew this secret place of his might be the perfect way to ask her more questions. Cases like this would also offer him experience he would need if he started his own private detective or bodyguard service later. He still hesitated, since he had never allowed anyone inside before.

"I promise you, I'll never tell anyone what your place looks like." She looked trustworthy, adding a trait he didn't expect, and one he had a hard time fighting.

Shawn knew better, but knew she needed someone to help her. "Okay, but only for a minute. I need to get you home before everyone starts asking about you. This building is old, and it doesn't have an elevator."

"You're kidding me."

Walking to the door leading inside his place, he paused. "It'll be interesting to see how my lady likes you."

"What lady? You said you weren't married."

Shawn soon opened the door as Lucy raced to him.

"Wow, you have a great dog."

"Yes, she keeps me company and never complains, except when I'm late getting home. Like I said, it's not much. Make yourself at home while I take her outside for a quick run. I'll be back soon."

"Okay, take your time. I think I'll lie on the couch over there for a minute."

Lucy tugged on his leg. "Okay, girl, I understand." He turned to face Kristina, who was already walking toward the couch. Her butt twitched in front of him. Damn, he had to remember who she was—the daughter of one of the directors. "I'll not be long."

###

Kristina felt very tired as she fluttered an eye open. While she hadn't slept the night before from worrying about her situation, she felt comfortable here, a place where she could hide from the world. She studied her surroundings without moving.

Her attention soon focused on a movement across from her. Dressed in sweat pants and a pull over, Shawn stretched from one position to another. His symmetrical movements resembled an art form, almost like ballet, but with a more focused message. While perhaps a form of Tia Chi or yoga, he moved liked a well oiled machine with every movement precise.

She assumed him to be around six feet tall and not much older than she was. He was not bulky, which was great in her opinion. His body stretched easily into the different poses, highlighting his great flexibility. While he had nice well-toned muscles, what caught her attention, as he moved around in his workout was his great abs.

She wondered how he had gotten into the bodyguard type business. The martial arts type movements answered her questions on his ability to handle himself. She would love to see him in action sometime. While she had several boyfriends during her life, many times these were simply guys she knew that were connected to her parents. The last one was almost fifteen years older than her. They had sex several times, but it never felt right, or close to it. He wasn't nearly in as good a shape as this guy in front of her.

As she watched, his movements changed to more forceful thrusts and punches. Almost like an aerobic exercise, he repeated the movements over and over. As the light above him highlighted his body, glistening off the sweat soaking his body now, she wondered if she would ever have a guy in such shape making love to her, and especially since she was soon going to be considered damaged goods. She had heard how guys talk about a girl with baggage which is what they really referred to as a baby. Yes, she wanted a family later, but much later. At twenty-five, she had only finished college a few years ago.

When visions of her dad invaded her thoughts, she lost the thrill of watching Shawn performing in front of her. Her dad wouldn't like what he would hear. She had no name to give him, and frankly she knew she might not ever know. She couldn't ask everyone on the boat to take a DNA test, could she? With a quick head count estimate of around fifty people, the list could be narrowed to around thirty plus men, and some of these were very old men who were on the board of directors. The scandal would be enormous, and she didn't think her dad wouldn't allow it.

Perhaps someone like Shawn was her best chance in finding out who it was. Many of the men she knew, and she had often talked to them at parties before. There were a few sons of the directors on the yacht that night. While several were too young for her, those would be the ones worth checking out. Some jerky little bastard could be responsible. She would make sure Shawn checked them out first.

While she watched Shawn switch his routine to a smoother, slower form, even his cooling down movements heated her passions. She knew she had gone too long without sex. Well, at least sex she remembered, or enjoyed. Being raped gave her chills of what might have happened. She wanted to be in control. She couldn't let one jerk ruin her life.

As Shawn finished his exercise, he walked over toward her. "I didn't know you were watching me."

She rose on her elbows to address him. "I can tell you're really into martial arts of some kind. Your movements looked almost poetic."

"My teacher will be proud to hear you say so. He always pushes me to improve."

"I was thinking, for a bodyguard you're a little small, don't you think?"

"Bulk size does have its advantage, but I think it's smarter to use your brain these days. I have the beef on my team when it's needed."

With a little effort, Kristina rose higher on her elbows. "How long have I been sleeping?"

"It's close to five, so I think about two or three hours."

The time sent tremors through her body since she would soon have to face her father. She could only hope he had a late office meeting, or some function he had to attend tonight. The fear must have shown on her face, as Shawn kneeled closer to her. His smell, which she thought would be all bad odors, surprised her. His scent carried a raw masculine allure, while his radiating body heat mesmerized her for several seconds.

As she started to refocus, she witnessed deep-brown eyes studying her before he asked, "Are you going to be okay?"

"Yes, give me a minute." She couldn't admit the effect he had on her. A relationship with him would be out of the question, but she could dream, couldn't she?

"Maybe the pregnancy is creating some chemical imbalances in you. You really should see your doctor."

"I'm sure I will soon, but for now, however, I need to decide how to tell my dad. He's going to hit the fucking ceiling."

"I can't say that I blame him, since he'll want to know who's responsible."

"That's something . . . I cannot give him. Since you agreed to help me, I need you to find out who did this."

She watched Shawn pull a chair from a small table over closer to her. "I'll do my best. Of course, you know the more information I have, the better chance I have. Are you prepared to tell me everything?"

"That depends on how much I can trust you."

"Trust is something we have to develop. It doesn't happen overnight."

"I really don't have much choice. Damn, life isn't fair!"

"It never is. I can attest to that."

Kristina wondered about his story and his background, but had to concentrate on her own. "I don't know where to start, and we don't have much time tonight."

"I can be a good listener. I'm going to make some coffee. Would you like some?" He stood and walked to the small area functioning as his kitchen.

"Yes, black and strong."

She watched him smile, as he turned to speak. "I knew there was a reason I liked you."

###

Shawn reached for a pad to take notes on. He knew

to go slow, or she would spook easily. "I'll do what I can to find the guy responsible, but first you should remember that I work for your father and many of the people on the company yacht."

"I know. I think your duties extend to the families of the executives at the company."

"They do. As you know, I'm often asked to provide security for family members. In your case, Mr. Lyons specifically asked me to take care of you after you contacted me when I was in his office."

"I'm sorry about embarrassing you, but I was scared you were telling him things already."

"As long as you know I'm walking a delicate line, I'll keep everything in confidence. The company, I'm sure, doesn't want a scandal anymore than you do." Shawn waited for her to acknowledge his concerns.

"Okay, I'm going to trust you, but if you burn me, I'll get even."

"I have no reason to tell anything simply to hurt you."

"Fair enough. Where do you want to start?"

"After the test today, I think we can agree you're pregnant. And as I understand, you don't remember having sex with anyone for a while."

"So far you're on target." He watched her eyes for any giveaway signs as she spoke.

"If the night on the cruise is assumed to be the only night in question, I think we should start with it . . . and from the beginning." Shawn leaned back in his chair as he prepared to do nothing but listen and take notes. He wrote the first one to himself regarding obtaining a full list of passengers.

Kristina bit her lip as she began. "I went on this

cruise because my parents made me. They thought it would be good for my image, and I think my dad would like to see me get back with Jeff. In a way, it would be good for me, I guess, but he's still too old for me, don't you think? I mean, he's like almost forty now."

"Jeff appears to be a nice guy. I'm not sure age has much to do with it, but it's something every couple needs to decide on their own. Just to check, how long has it been since you saw each other?"

"I went to his condo like maybe three or four months ago. I knew he was already seeing this new girl. I didn't think it would last, and I didn't mind being with him one more time. The sex we had was almost mechanical. I think I deserve better treatment, don't you?"

Shawn tried to remain calm as he talked sex with a beautiful woman in his apartment. It had been a long time for him also. "So, we can absolutely rule out him being the father from an earlier . . . night."

"Yes."

"I guess we need to get back to the night of the cruise."

Kristina sank back into the cushions on the sofa. "I felt like if I was forced to go, I might as well enjoy myself. As you may have heard, the company was celebrating a major contract, and a lot of champagne was offered to me. Everyone wanted to propose a toast for this or for that."

Shawn had heard about it. He normally would've been onboard, but he had other duties the night of the cruise. Someone had launched a cyber attack on the main headquarters, and downloaded access codes to the doors and secured areas. The hackers must have known the real brains would be on the corporate yacht and saw it as their best chance to break in. He stood in the main gate all night with extra guards recruited on a last minute notice. Without such beefed up security, who knows what might have happened.

She looked at him as he scribbled notes. "Eventually I felt sick and kind of weak. I don't remember much after drinking except having Jeff help me downstairs to a cabin. I woke the next morning feeling like shit. One of your men drove me home. The rest of the guests had left the night before."

Shawn tapped the pencil on the pad, as he waited for her to continue. "I know what you're thinking. It had to be Jeff, right?"

"It sounds logical to suspect him at this point."

"I heard later about how he had danced with his new girlfriend all night. The chances are slim it's him. He doesn't have to drug me. We've made love before, and I'm sure he knows we could be on again at some time."

While it made sense, he scribbled a note to check further into it.

"The yacht had many people on it, but many of them were my dad's age or older. I think the only possibility is some of the sons of other board members."

Again Shawn entered a note. It could be the crazy exploits of a crazy young guy on board, and especially if he was allowed to drink champagne with the adults. "Do you remember any of these guys' names, or did you have any contact with them you remember?"

"Nothing really. I had a few stares here and there

for sure, but nothing out of the ordinary."

"You said you slept late the next morning, and that everyone had deserted you."

"I'm sure someone tried to wake me but gave up. One of the security guys was left to drive me back to my parent's place."

"I'm sure I can find out who the driver was. Are you suspicious of the driver in any way?"

"He acted normal and polite. I barely remember it, but I do remember having a headache, which I thought was from the champagne."

"Understandable. Did you notice anything different about your clothing, or notice any body pains or bruises you might not be able to explain otherwise?"

"Nothing really. If I was raped, the attacker, at least, was gentle with me."

Shawn swallowed before he asked the next question. "Did you see any signs of fluids or discolorations anywhere?"

"I don't remember. I went home and had a shower. A housekeeper takes care of our washing, etcetera, in our condo."

Shawn noticed how she kept referring to her place. He would think at her age she would be on her own by now. "It might be hard for me to ask your housekeeper some questions like this. It might be good for you to talk to her."

"I'll see what I can do, but we have a full staff of people working for us."

"This will give me enough to work on for a while. Let me know how it goes with your father. If I'm to keep this between us, I don't need to be blindsided by questions."

"I will." He watched her glance around. "I can see why you like it here. You have no one around to bother you."

"Yes, that's kind of nice. Now, let me take you home." He hoped bringing her to his place wouldn't get out. This wasn't a good idea. As he reached for her hand to help her stand, it felt so natural in his—too natural.

Chapter 5

Kristina entered the front door of her condo and saw her mother waiting on her with panic stretching her face into a strange convulsion. "I've been trying to call you. Where have you been?" Her mother glanced over her shoulder before taking Katrina's arm and pulling her to the activity room, which was off to one side of the vestibule. "Hurry, before your father sees you."

"What's going on?"

"The maid found your test strip and told your father."

"She had no right to search through my stuff!"

"Right or no right, your father has been trying to call you."

Kristina's heart beat faster as she struggled with another onset of dizziness which was a strange feeling she hadn't experienced until recently. "I turned my phone off and wanted to be left alone to think."

"He heard Shawn, the head of security, had taken you shopping. He's trying to reach him now."

"He dropped me off a few minutes ago."

"Damn, that means he'll be looking for you any minute."

A loud knock on the door announced his presence as he didn't stop to wait on an answer. His face flashed a bright deep red. She had seen such a look before. "There you are. Shawn told me he had been with you all day, and dropped you off here a few minutes ago. Do you want to tell me what you were doing with him today?"

"Dad, he was my driver."

"I know who he is. I'm not stupid. But . . . what I want to know is where he drove you today. And I bet it has something to do with this." He presented the pregnancy kit.

"Mom told me a few minutes ago that the maid found it. She had no right in searching my things!"

"She apologized, but she said she found it putting away some of your clothes. She thought I should know, and I'm glad she confided in me, which is something I wish my own daughter would do."

"Look at you. Do you think I really want to talk to you about this right now?"

"This is one time your partying ways have caught up with you. I hope you're happy."

"Dad, I don't sleep around!"

"Really, then tell me who's going to be my new son-in-law?"

"I don't know who the father is, and I'm not planning on marrying anyone!"

Kristina watched her father extend his hands into the air above him in frustration. "I do my best to try to raise you right and show respect for the family, and this is how I'm paid back."

"Dad, you might as well know."

"Know what?"

"I think I was raped."

The words appeared to dazzle him. With his ragging attitude silenced, he staggered. "And . . . you're just now telling me this!"

"Dad, I don't have many answers yet. I went looking for them today. Based on what I think now, I was given a date rape drug."

"Have you contacted the police?"

"No, I have no proof, other than I'm pregnant. What do you think they'll do with that?" Kristina felt another wave of nausea overtaking her as the world swirled around her.

###

Kristina woke in her bed later with a warm cloth on her forehead. She pried open an eye to gain her bearings, and saw her mother rush to her from one side. "You're awake."

"What happened?"

A man on the other side of the bed reached for her hand. "My name's Dr. Davison, your father called me to come check on you." He leaned forward to stare into her eyes. "You passed out. It happens to some women when they first become pregnant."

Kristina glanced at her father. With his rage slightly diminished, he had tears in his eyes. "I'm sorry, baby. Forgive me."

She closed her eyes again, knowing that this would only be the beginning. When she opened them again she saw Shawn on the far side of the room. What was he doing here?

Her father walked over to Shawn. "I think she'll be okay now. I really appreciate you helping me get her to her room. I'm much too old to do any lifting these days. We need to talk tomorrow morning, since I'll need your help in containing this. I also want you to see to it Kristina stays out of site and for you to personally take her wherever she needs to go. The rest of the guys on the board will have to settle for someone else who works for you for a while."

"You know you can count on me, sir. I'm glad you called me to help."

As Shawn turned to leave, her father walked to him and shook his hand. "I'm sure you know none of this leaves this room."

"Yes, sir. I understand fully."

"Good, be here by eight and we'll talk over breakfast."

Kristina watched him move closer to her and smile. "I'm sure everything will work out for you. Get some rest."

"Thanks for all of your help." She knew she would worry all night about what her father had asked him. She would be sure to make the breakfast meeting tomorrow morning.

Chapter 6

Shawn cleared his throat as he walked in the next morning. While he had been buzzed in, no one was waiting for him as he wandered into the Sutherland penthouse. With the show of wealth dominating his imagination, he studied the art work paid for by the sweat and brains of many young, unknown workers.

Shawn had studied the situation all night after he had made many calls to the two men who had worked the cruise, but for now he disclosed nothing about the alleged rape. While he wanted to believe Kristina, he simply had to go on the facts as he knew them.

Lawson shouted into a cell phone as Shawn rounded the corner. "Kelly, I know this is quick notice, but I want this taken care of now! I want this emergency meeting called this afternoon. Let me know who can't make it."

Shawn knew Kelly Bower, the corporate secretary for the company, who had made it known several times recently that she would like to return to private legal practice. However, he knew the company would miss her if she did, since she was the one person who managed to work out compromises when problems occurred on the board.

Lawson dropped his phone in a pocket. "I'm glad you got here early. We need to talk."

"Yes, sir. I've been doing some research over the night."

"Good, I hoped you would. Let's take some

breakfast out on the patio."

After walking out to the patio, Shawn watched one of the house staff preparing a table. This was unusual treatment for him to be invited to eat with a member of the board. He often had to stand in the background and watch the rich guys and their families enjoy expensive foods and wines.

However, he knew why since Lawson wanted to know who got his daughter pregnant, and he wanted it done quietly. While he remained a public figure, known for his financial genius, it was his wife who dominated the society pages. Shawn knew that public image was extremely important to him and his family.

"Please have a seat." Lawson pointed to one of the two seats at the table.

"Thank you. This is highly unusual."

Lawson smiled. "I think my daughter has placed a lot of confidence in you, and to be honest, I find myself also needing to do so."

"I understand the situation, sir."

"Good, I'm glad we have an understanding." One staff worker suddenly walked out to bring several platters to the table. Lawson's eyes and facial gestures stressed how much he wanted their conversations to be private.

Lawson glanced at the food. "I wasn't sure what you liked to eat, so I had the kitchen prepare a combination of offerings. I'm sure you'll find something you might like." He glanced at the server. "Thank you. We have some business we need to discuss, please hold all calls for a while."

"Yes, sir." The waiter glanced at Shawn with a questioning look on his face, but left quickly.

Lawson wasted no time in getting down to business. "Kristina says she was raped." He paused to open a file Shawn had worked on the night before. "She also said it happened on our company yacht." Lawson's fist pounded on the table. "I need to know who!"

"I know how you feel. I have a complete list of everyone who attended the celebration cruise." He handed the list to Lawson.

"Most of these men are my age, with the exception of the workers on board and a few sons of the board members." Lawson glanced at the list as his hand quivered with anger too hard to hide.

"I think it'll be easy to isolate the ones who need scrutiny. I'll start full interviews today." Shawn tried to remain as calm as possible, hoping to keep Lawson under control as well.

"Good, I'm calling a board meeting this afternoon, since they need to be aware of what has happened. I don't know how long it'll be until word of this reaches the press, so I'll need your help in containing this as long as possible."

"I have a good staff working for me, but it might be good to allow me to hire a few extra men."

"Not a problem. Send me a request and I'll approve it immediately."

"You'll have it in a few hours." Shawn stretched back in his seat. "How is Kristina this morning?"

"Her mother's with her. She's trying to talk Kristina into having an abortion as quick as possible."

Shawn's face gave away his thoughts on abortion.

"I see you must be one of those who don't believe in abortions, which is interesting being a guy of your age."

"I try to keep my thoughts to myself, but since you asked, let me say my mother was pressured hard into having an abortion. I, for one, am very thankful she didn't listen to those who would not have allowed me a chance to be born."

"I understand your point, but we have much at stake with this."

"In all due respect, I hope your grandson or granddaughter understands."

He watched Lawson shift sideways in his seat. "I'm not in disagreement with you, but my daughter was raped. Right now, I don't want to accept the fact some man forced himself on her and had his way with her. Damn, this is my little girl we're talking about!"

"I hear you. The first thing we need to determine is who this is. I also know you have your daughter's best interest at heart. I don't know her well, but from spending some time with her yesterday, I think she's a very nice woman."

"Thank you for saying so." Lawson leaned forward. "Did she tell you anything else I need to know? I mean, did she have any idea who this might me."

"Your daughter's confused about what happened, and what she should do. I see her as very brave, but scared. Don't worry; she's concerned about anyone finding out, which is why I think she called me."

"She's a great daughter, but as you surely know, she can have her moments. Many kids today are too wild. I know she wants to enjoy life, which I hear from her often, but she has also lived a sheltered life."

Shawn felt torn between telling all Kristina had

told him, and remaining in her confidence.

"Shawn, the meeting starts at three this afternoon. Find out as much as you can, and be there about thirty minutes early to bring me up to date."

Shawn stood. "Tell Kristina I hope she's feeling better today, and to call me anytime she needs to go anywhere."

"I will. She trusts you. She asked about you last night after you left."

Shawn smiled, but knew her concerns. She had to want to know what he had disclosed. He felt sure she would contact him soon.

###

Kristina locked her door. She wasn't going to be pushed into a decision, but she also had no intention of being a mother. The thought had never crossed her mind before. Still, the images on the signs and posters haunted her all night. She wasn't a baby killer. Their message was so cruel, so uncalled for.

After sliding into a seat of a small desk in her bedroom where she kept her personal computer, she clicked on one medical site after another. She needed some answers. What all was involved in an abortion? Would it hurt? Would it affect her future chances of getting pregnant?

Many sites offered their services and bragged about how private their practice was. Sure, she sneered, exactly like what she experienced the day before. Eventually, she read the sites pushed by the pro-life side. At first she ignored them, but curiosity persisted. She cried at the end of one video she watched. She had to admit it; she carried a baby in her stomach. What was she to do?

She heard a loud knock on her door, followed by her mother's voice. "Please open the door. We need to talk!"

She didn't want to, but she knew that she couldn't hide forever. She had, however, made her mind up to wait to make a decision. What she really wanted to do was talk to Shawn. She closed the windows on her computer and walked to the door.

While her mother was dressed in a new business suit and had her makeup on, she still looked pale. "I heard your father has called a meeting of the board for this afternoon to address your situation."

"Oh no, I don't want everyone to know this!"

"I think your father wants to make sure it doesn't get outside the board. He's afraid word will break soon."

"Why? I should be the only one who knows this."

"He had Shawn, the head of security, come by this morning where he could give him instructions on finding out who's responsible. He also asked him to hire additional people to help."

"I see." She hoped Shawn didn't tell her father everything, since he had promised to keep some secrets. "What did Shawn tell him about our trip yesterday?"

"I'm not sure they discussed it at all, since I think they concentrated on finding out who did this to you."

"I don't need my dad going off like this. Don't I have some say in how to handle my life?"

"I'm sorry, but I knew you would want to know what was going on."

"I need to talk to Shawn before he does this. I don't want my name all over the tabloids."

"I think your father wants the same, which is why he's using Shawn."

"Still, I want to talk to him."

"That won't be a problem. Your father also instructed Shawn to personally be available to keep you safe from any crowds, or media attacks which might come up. Personally, I think we need to stay inside until this blows over and we can work out details on this abortion."

"Mom, I'm not so sure about this."

"What?"

"I need some time to think about this. I don't want to be known as a *baby killer*." Kristina bit her lip. "I need to talk to Shawn before this meeting."

"I'm not sure—"

"This is my life, and I do have a say in it." Kristina stood and walked over to her phone. "I want to know what he knows before he tells the world." She kept her eye on her mother as she hunted for his number on the card he gave her earlier.

He answered on the second ring. "This is Shawn."

"Yes, how are you?" She really didn't care, but asked out of years of pressure to act polite in all settings. Still, she didn't wait for an answer as she continued. "This is Kristina and we need to talk."

"Okay. Your father has me working hard today."

"I heard all about the board meeting." She glanced at her mother. "I want a minute alone."

Her mother started to object until Kristina dropped the phone, prepared to do battle. "Don't do anything stupid, Kristina."

"It's a little late for that, don't you think?"

Her mother paraded out as Kristina closed and

locked the door. As an added layer of protection she walked to the bathroom. "I thought you said you would keep what I told you in confidence."

"I haven't said a word to him you told me, other than what he has already figured out. You have to remember, he's one of my bosses."

"I knew you would say that. Where does that leave me?"

"I'm gathering information as discreetly as I can, and it's not easy. It's your father who wants to bring it to a head this afternoon. I have no control of his actions."

"I know my father. He's more upset than he lets on. Why is he asking for a board meeting to hang out my dirty laundry?"

"He wants help in determining who raped you. What I think he really wants is for everyone to submit to a DNA test."

"Damn, I'm sure his request will go over well. I've been thinking about it. One of the rich, arrogant sons of one of the board members probably did it. And . . . I can just hear him bragging about it. The bastard. "

"You could be right."

"I know my dad won't tell me everything that happens today. After the meeting, I want to know everything." Kristina thought about it, running a plan over in her mind. "I don't want my dad around when we talk. I often go to the Manhattan Club on Wednesday nights, but many of my friends are going to a private party tonight. I want you to take me there to eat. I'll not stay long, but I want you to tell me what happened on the way there and back."

"Whatever you wish."

"I hope that I can trust you."

"You can."

She ended the call without saying another word, as she realized he wasn't the one she should be mad at. It was the actions of her father who would cause her hell. Still, trust was something she had a hard time with, and something she knew she should work on. She needed someone to help her during this ordeal. Someone she could trust completely. Could that be Shawn?

Shawn stepped into the boardroom and scanned the area, since he wanted to make damn sure the room was bug free before the meeting. These skills he had learned while advancing through the ranks made him an expert at what he did. While he knew his work went unnoticed most of the time, he knew it was supposed to be that way.

Lawson walked in soon and shut the doors behind him. "I'm glad you came early. I need to know what you've discovered."

"I really need more time, but I've been working the list of attendees you already have. Between the small group of young guys on the yacht and the staff, we have around fourteen suspects. If you add the eleven members of the board, you have twenty five. I have only had a chance to briefly talk to the crew aboard and my staff regarding anything suspicious they saw."

"What are you telling them about your questioning?"

"For now, I have to be vague, which makes it hard to find out much."

"I understand. If word of this gets out, it'll have a major impact on this company. These are professional men, and they will know why I'm doing this. It's your job to help us resolve this quietly. Someone had to have seen something."

Kelly walked in as they turned to face the opening door. "There you are. I still don't know why you called this meeting. You can at least tell the company attorney what's going on."

Lawson looked at Shawn and then at Kelly. "Have a seat, you're not going to like this."

Shawn excused himself as he rechecked the room and prepared to greet the men on the board when they arrived.

Later, Shawn glanced at Kelly, who continued to shake her head long after Lawson quit talking to her. She remained seated which was unusual, as she loved to chat with the board members when they arrived.

Finally, with all accounted for, including Kelly who was also a board member, Lawson stood. "Men, I hate to disturb your day, but last night I learned some disturbing news that if not handled quickly will greatly damage our reputation as a company and . . . on a personal note has caused me a lot of anger I hope I can hold in." With his words growing louder as he spoke, he stopped for a minute. "I think we should hear from Shawn, who I think everyone here knows."

Nothing like being put on the spot. Shawn walked to the head of the table. "There's a reason Mr. Sutherland is upset. It appears that on the celebration cruise we all enjoyed last month, his daughter was raped after being given a date rape drug of some kind."

Every board member started to ask questions at

once. Shawn raised his hands. "Please let me continue." He waited on them to hush.

"I understand how upset Mr. Sutherland is, and I'm sure everyone here would feel the same way if it was their daughter." He paused to allow the words to sink in. "Here are the facts as we know them. First, yesterday we received confirmation that Kristina is pregnant. The night in question is the night of the cruise where she passed out."

Jeff, the CEO of the company, stood. "It sounds like a lot of speculation. Why is this just now coming to light? And let me say I remember the night. In fact, as many of you might remember, I helped her downstairs to one of the cabins. I'll assure you; I left her sleeping it off, and I was only gone for a few minutes."

Shawn looked at Jeff. "Sir, I don't think anyone is accusing you."

Jeff snapped back. "Okay, then who is it you're accusing?"

"I don't have information to accuse anyone."

Luckily Lawson stood back up in his defense. "We had many people on board. I've asked Shawn to do some investigation, and he'll continue to do so. I know what a scandal like this will do to us, and I hope to keep this quiet until the person responsible is identified."

Jeff looked at Lawson, and lowered his voice as he spoke directly at Shawn. "So what is it you're proposing—that we all take a DNA test?" Shawn raised his hand, as if to ask for permission to speak. "What is it?" Jeff asked as he glanced back at Shawn.

Shawn forced his words to make them spaced and

controlled. "I have a list of all of the men on board. In additional to every member of the board, we had a full crew, and several sons of members of the board."

The reaction was immediate from all three members with sons on the boat. "Not my son."

Lawson turned to Kelly, as if for legal advice. "I know demanding a DNA sample will be hard to ask for, but for those who want to, it will narrow the list for us to investigate. Am I correct in presenting it this way?"

"Absolutely, we don't want to accuse anyone, especially without proof. This would have to be strictly voluntarily submitted."

Shawn's grandfather had remained quiet during the meeting until now. "You mean all of us?"

Kelly regained control of the meeting. "I know many of the men on the board are like old enough to be her grandfather, which is why this has to be voluntary. If we ask for specific people it might get us in trouble with libeling someone. This should be just a means of clearing anyone's name upfront."

The three board members with the sons who attended understood, and reacted first, as David Swafford spoke for the group. "I think our sons have nothing to hide, and I'm sure they'll be more than willing to give a DNA sample to clear their name. I would think the people to concentrate on would be the crew."

Shawn spoke quickly to cover his point. "Since they're employees, I don't think we'll have any problems obtaining samples from them. If they don't comply, we'll have grounds to dismiss them, and perhaps turn the matter over to the police."

Brent stood to gain attention. "I know this is unfortunate, and I feel for my friend, Lawson, but shouldn't Kristina simply have an abortion quietly, and save us all some embarrassing moments?"

Lawson glared at the other members. "This is still sinking in for both me and Kristina. She hasn't made a decision on the abortion yet, but I know it's being considered."

Brent shook his head. "Surely she doesn't intend to keep the baby."

Shawn couldn't resist, in spite of the fight it would cause later with his grandfather. "We all know an abortion is the taking of a life, and some people would make an argument its wrong, no matter how it was caused. Each person has to make their own decision."

If only the members of the board knew the truth. Shawn fought to control the urge to tell all, and get it out of his system. But . . . what would he do next? He needed this job for now. Not much longer, true, but for at least another year or two to have enough money to start his own firm. He also realized how the scandal might jeopardize his own future as he hoped to receive many referrals from these men who also served on many other boards. Still, he stood his own until his grandfather had a seat.

Jeff stood to take control of the meeting. "I understand how everyone feels. At first I thought this was wrong to discuss here, but I think I understand why Lawson called this meeting. The media would have a heyday with it. As such, I trust everything we discuss here will not leave this room." He turned toward Shawn. "I'm depending on you to keep a lid on this as you gather information and find out who's responsible."

Turning to the men with sons, he continued, "I'm also sure you'll instruct your sons to not discuss this with anyone." The three board members shook their head yes without saying a word. Finally, Jeff turned to Lawson. "My good friend, I want you to know how much I, as I'm sure the rest of the board, feel for you during this time. You can count on us to help you in any way we can. I especially hate it for Kristina, since we've dated on and off for a long time. She's a very special girl." Jeff appeared to be fighting back emotions he didn't want the others to see.

As the meeting ended, Shawn caught the intense stare coming from his grandfather, the man who did everything possible to have his mother abort him many years ago. *How could he be so cruel?* Still, he caught a glimmer of a smile as he watched him wink at him. This confused him, as it sent a message of being proud of him. *But if so, why?* Was it for standing his ground? He had to talk to him again soon.

Chapter 7

Shawn rushed to his office and shut the door, since he needed to make some calls. Tomorrow morning he would start interviewing everyone on the staff. While his work would be stressful, knowing what was at stake, he wanted to be prepared as he accessed the personnel files stored on the company data base that he had clearance to use.

His phone rang. "This is Shawn."

"What did they say at the meeting?" He recognized the tension in Kristina's voice immediately.

"Your dad's asking for DNA samples from everyone, but it's being asked for on a volunteer basis for now."

"So the whole company knows about what happened."

"It was emphasized that this wasn't to be discussed outside the board room."

"Do you really believe that shit? Some of my friends are also kids of members of the board, or related in some way."

"I'm to interview everyone who worked on the yacht the night in question. I'm pulling the personnel files right now so that I can be prepared for them."

"What about the sons of the board members?"

"The board members assured everyone they'll be submitting DNA samples."

"We need to talk about this. I'm not so sure I want to have the baby submit DNA samples, or whatever they have to do."

"What?"

"This is like getting out of hand. I don't want people to sneer at me and think I'm some kind of trashy girl who can't handle her partying."

"I'm here to help you any way I can. I just need to know what you want me to do." Shawn waited on a long pause.

"We'll talk more tonight after you escort me to dinner."

"It will be good to talk later. Who are you going to be dining with?"

"I've reserved a private area. This is the only way I know I can discuss this with you without my father standing over me, or people listening in."

"Not a problem. I know a way of getting in and out of the Manhattan Club without being seen by many."

"Good, I'll be ready to be picked up at seven."

"I'll be on time." The phone line died without a goodbye. She was going to have dinner with him, but she left it clear that she still considered him hired help. No problem, that is what he was, and this was still a job; a demanding job, but still a job. Still . . . she was beautiful.

###

Kristina paused by the door of her condo. Since she had planned to keep her escort from coming up, she needed to meet him downstairs as soon as he arrived. While she wanted to keep him away from her dad, so that the two would have no time to compare notes, she knew they would be talking during the day. She wanted this over.

Her dad surprised her when he walked over to her

as she waited on him to arrive. "Are you sure you want to go out?"

"I can't stay inside all of my life. I want to see some of my friends. Don't worry since I'll have Shawn with me tonight."

"I hope you understand that he can't be your personal bodyguard forever."

"I understand, but I was told he was to provide me extra coverage for now."

"Yes, the company has a special interest in you."

"I'll be back late tonight." She knew she was causing problems, but tough, she didn't ask for this. She decided to walk out the door and wait downstairs on Shawn. Her dad didn't say another word as she left.

After reaching the ground level of the elevator, she walked toward the front door and allowed the doorman to open it for her. When she stepped into the cool evening breeze looking for Shawn, she didn't expect what she received. She watched a door to a car parked across the street open and a strange man, much too far away to be identified, stand and obviously shoot her a bird. He then pointed a finger at her and shouted something undistinguishable, but she assumed profanity before returning to his car.

As the car, more of a SUV hybrid, sped away, she decided it would be better to step back inside to wait. What in the hell was that? Her phone rang. Thinking it was Shawn, she answered, "Hi, are you close?"

"Yes, I'm close. I heard about your problem, you cheap fucking bitch. And . . . you'll keep seeing me until you get your abortion and end this."

Kristina snapped the phone shut. This gravelly voice had to belong to the guy she watched speed off seconds ago. She checked the caller ID, which showed no data. She had to show this to Shawn and hope the company had to have a way to find out who it was, but it looked like she would be without a phone until tomorrow morning since she wouldn't answer it again. Damn it!

As the doorman stood beside her, he asked, "Are you okay?"

"Did you see the guy across the street yelling at me?"

He acted stunned as he glanced through the glass door to the outside. "Which guy?"

"Never mind, just some jerk on the street." Her body shook as the event fully registered. Perhaps she did need to stay inside. No, she had a bodyguard with her tonight, and the best one who worked for her dad's company.

Finally Shawn stepped out of a limo which he had pulled in front of the door. He looked clean cut, but in the traditional black suit required by the company. She waited on him to reach the door before she signaled to the doorman she wanted to go out.

A pleasant smile greeted her. "I would have been glad to come up and get you."

"I didn't want to face my dad any longer. We need to talk as soon as we get inside. I had a guy across the street yell at me."

Shawn immediately stepped in front of her as if to shelter her. "Where?"

"He's gone now." After Shawn ushered her to the back seat of the limo and climbed in behind her, she handed him her phone. "He also called me."

Shawn accepted the phone, and checked the ID

like she had. "I can have the phone company check the records, but I think it will be one of those disposable phones. Everyone knows how to get one for harassment these days."

She decided to give him some instructions after they drove toward the Manhattan club. "I don't think many people will be there tonight. I just had to get away from my parents for a while. I also want to know what all happened today." She wanted to check her lipstick as they were only a few blocks away, but continued. "After I make a few rounds to greet whoever is there, I want to go to the private dining room I reserved. I want you to join me there later. Until then, everyone will recognize you as my bodyguard. This will send a strong message to whoever yelled at me that I have you with me, and also not alert everyone to the fact that we have some talking to do."

Shawn appeared to understand. "This is always an exclusive club. We should have no problem there since I know their security staff very well."

As they pulled in front of the entrance and stepped outside, Kristina watched a SUV much like the one she witness earlier speed past them. Was it the same one? She blinked her eyes as the vehicle disappeared down the street. While it was too late to point to it for Shawn, she knew she was becoming paranoid about it all. She needed a drink.

Minutes later, she walked into the club where the place buzzed with light talk as people moved around inside. She left Shawn by the door. "I'll not be long."

"Take your time. I want to check out this phone call. I'll be right outside."

Kristina smiled at him, and hoped he could get some details on who called her. She hoped there would not be many people she knew inside the club so she could disappear to the private dining room quickly. She only wanted to make a few contacts in case her father asked who she saw.

As a small crowd walked next to the viewing area off the patio, she walked toward them, but suddenly stopped. One of the boys she recognized. He had been on the cruise the night she had been drugged. His name was Josh, and his father who was on the board often played golf with her dad. His eyes focusing on her told her he knew of the meeting.

As several others smiled at her, his glare intensified. She had no intention of bringing her sordid night out into the discussion. Coming here was a bad idea after all. She should have listened to her dad.

She waved at the crowd and pointed to her watch, trying to indicate she was late for her dinner arrangements. She was the only one who knew she was going to have diner alone. Well, not totally alone, since Shawn would be there.

As she turned to walk away, she saw another old friend who she had studied with often in college. "Hello, BreAnna."

"Oh, hello. I haven't seen you in a while." BreAnna wore a short black dress and looked fantastic. She must have lost some weight, with her legs much more shapely than she remembered. That must be why she was showing them off.

"I've been around. What have you been up to?"

"I decided to go to law school."

"Really!"

"Yes, my new boyfriend is going there, and he talked me into it last year." BreAnna waved across the room at Josh.

Kristina felt sick. Word would get back to BreAnna soon. She didn't think Josh would be the one slipping her a drug, but he was one of the three young guys on the yacht. Having a steady girlfriend made it less likely. "I'm sorry, but I have to leave. We're eating in a private room tonight."

"Hummm, it sounds like you have a new secret boyfriend. You have to tell me about him later. Call me."

As she watched Josh move toward them, she had no time to explain. "I'll call you later." Kristina turned and walked to the outside hallway.

She saw Shawn pressing a phone close to his ear as he smiled. "It was as I assumed. There's no way to know who called you. You'll need to get a new number."

"Okay, I'll call later tonight. Are you hungry?"

"I'm always hungry. Are you inviting me to eat with you?"

"We need to talk, and I don't want to eat by myself. Come on. Let's go to our dining room." Kristina moved quickly past the members inside, and breathed easier once the door was closed to the private dining room. "Shawn, would you like something to drink?"

"I can't. I'm still on duty."

"I understand, but I wouldn't say anything."

"Thanks, but I think black coffee would be good enough for me."

Kristina turned to the waiter. "Coffee for him, and

a glass of pinot noir for me. Also, we're in no hurry tonight."

"No problem. Let me know when you want to order." He turned and left, leaving them in an awkward moment of silence.

"It's not going to get any easier, is it?" She allowed her shoulders to droop. The sound of the voice on the phone replayed over and over.

"Being a limited number of people on the yacht, I think we'll be able to narrow the list quickly. How this plays out in the media and the courts may be a different thing."

She hadn't thought much about a trial which might be involved. Would she have to make a spectacle out of herself in the courts? She had heard stories about this before on the news. "I didn't think about all of this. Perhaps, I should simply have an abortion and tell everyone it was a mistake."

"The choice is always up to you, but I think you know my feelings on this."

Being able to shift her mind from her impending gloom to his words for a moment, she felt intrigued to know more about his story. "I really don't know much about you. Would you like to tell me why you're so headstrong on me not having an abortion?"

"This might be a little boring for you."

"Try me."

"My mother ran off with someone that my grandfather hated and saw as perfectly unacceptable for my mother. She soon became pregnant with me. Actually, grandfather was right about my father, since I've never seen him in my life. He disappeared as soon as he heard mom was pregnant, leaving her to fend on her own. Grandfather wouldn't help her at all, turning his back on her completely since she refused to have an abortion."

"I'm sorry. I can't believe my father would ever do that." Of course, she hadn't faced that crisis yet. Would her father also expect her to have one? Everything was happening so fast. "You appear to have turned out okay."

"Life wasn't easy for us. My mother worked many long hours, keeping us alive until she died about five years ago."

"I'm sorry to hear about your mom. And . . . you never heard from your dad?"

"Never. I know where he lives, but I have no intentions of ever seeing him."

"You mentioned a grandfather. Is he the only other relative you have?"

"Yes, that's it." Shawn paused. "Even when it gets as about as bad as it can get, I still know a life, any kind of life, is better than not having the chance to live. So . . . I think you know my opinion on abortions."

Kristina felt of her stomach, thinking about her unborn baby. Would it feel the same way? "You make a good case, but what about the life your mother could have had?"

She watched him smile. "Life was hard, but I don't think mom would have had it any other way."

Kristina wasn't expecting this. She wanted to ask if he was sure about this, but held her tongue. He had his convictions, and he wasn't trying to overpower her with them. He had a quiet strength she never recognized in other men she knew before. She studied his face. He wasn't too bad looking, and was really kind of nice in a rugged sort of way. But still . . . he was working in security, and a relationship with someone like that would never work. He had no prospects of being able to support her needs.

Shawn's posture remained firm as he waited patiently on her. While she had seen where he lived, she soon also wondered about other parts of his life. He appeared to work all of the time, and had no personal life, but that also meant he had no pressures of dealing with people like she had to. In a way she envied him.

Shawn leaned forward as if to whisper. "I know you want to know what happened today in the meeting."

Her mind cleared, as she focused on her own problems. "I still cannot believe my father would embarrass me in front of everyone."

"I think many fathers can identify with his actions. An attack on you could easily be conceived of as an attack on him. Since he cannot allow such, striking out the way he did is understandable. He demands answers, and he usually gets them. I hope you take what I'm saying confidentially."

"Sure."

"Your father expects people to do what he says. While he wants fast answers, I wish I had more time to conduct an investigation."

"Between you and me, I would prefer you did." She paused. "I saw one of the guys who was on the yacht a few minutes ago here in the club. You should have seen the look he gave me."

"Which guy?"

"His name is Josh, and I also ran into an old school mate of mine who's dating him now. With a steady girlfriend that might rule him out, but he must have been told about the meeting. I know of no other reason for him to stare at me like that."

"You're probably right about him knowing, since all of the board members with sons on board said they would ask their sons to submit DNA samples."

"I don't know. I was thinking earlier. If I got drugged, it could also be easy for a bartender to slip something in my drink."

"Yes, but a bartender will be a prime suspect, and many of these workers are very protective of their jobs. Still . . . tomorrow morning I'll start my interviews and try to get to the bottom of this." Shawn's face turned more compassionate, as he continued, "Can I ask you something . . . personal?"

A slight feeling of shock inched over her neck, as she straightened her back. "I suppose."

"I know this is a lot to hit you with, and you appear to be handing everything well, but I do have some connections with a rape crisis center if you need to talk to anyone."

His caring moment made her realize he had a true soft side. "As far as the actual rape, I try not to think about it. Since I remember nothing at all, I have no nightmares about it. I'm mad at what it will cost me. Perhaps I'll feel differently after it all sets in later."

"I guess being drugged has one slight benefit. So, you still cannot remember any details at all."

"I remember drinking champagne with everyone, and waking the next morning. That's it. What do you think he used on me?"

"I don't know, but I have an appointment with someone who might be able to help. Don't worry, it'll be confidential."

"I've heard about girls being put on the witness stand, and having to go through their entire sex life. Tell me I'll not have to go on the witness stand."

"I'm no lawyer, but you might be right."

Katrina felt the lumps in her throat. "I'm no virgin, but I don't sleep around. I've had a few affairs, and you might know that my longest ongoing one was with Jeff, but he has this new girlfriend, and we haven't seen each other for over four months now. I know I'm not four months pregnant. We used protection." *Ooops, she didn't mean to let that last part out and give details.*

"I'm not here to judge anyone. As the head of security, I see the affairs."

Kristina blinked her eyes, as she realized his admission. There was no telling what he knew. "I never thought much about it, but I do bet you have an interesting life and many stories to tell."

"I've learned to keep my mouth shut."

Katrina knew she wouldn't get any juicy stories out of him, but she wished she could, especially on Jeff's new girlfriend. She would work on it later. "I have no choice but to trust you, but I want no one to know what you know about me."

"Fully understood."

"That includes my dad."

"That puts me in a tight position, don't you think?"

"Yes, but I think you know the difference between being loyal to him, and respecting my privacy."

Shawn reached for his coffee. "I think we

understand each other."

Shawn enjoyed the meal with the slight feeling of a date adding to the night. However, he lived in the real world, and he knew his place and hers. After he called for the limo, knowing it would be waiting on him as he stepped outside, he walked out ahead of Kristina, a habit he had developed from working in security. When all appeared to be clear, he reached inside and helped her toward the limo.

When the shattering sound of a bottle crashing to one side of him startled him, he quickly glanced at the wall where a smoky vapor was escaping from the broken bottle. His first thoughts—acid. Since the limo was closer than returning to the entrance, he pulled Kristina toward the limo door. He heard woman screaming as another bottle crashed on the sidewalk not far from him. He didn't stop to look around since he had to get Kristina inside immediately.

Shawn slammed the door shut as the driver looked over the back seat. "What in the hell is this?"

"I don't know—drive!" He reached for his phone and dialed 911. He needed back up. "Yes, this is Shawn Davis, head of security for Lyon International. We're in front of the Manhattan Club and are under attack. I'm taking my client to safety, but will be back in about ten to fifteen minutes."

"We have already received a call on a disturbance there."

"Good, I'll be back soon." The limo quickly entered the street, and headed toward Fifth Avenue as he turned to Kristina. "Are you okay?"

"Oh shit, what the fuck was that?"

"I don't know yet, but it looks like someone was throwing bottles."

"Why?"

Shawn avoided a question impossible to answer. "I'll have you back to your place in a minute. Listen to me, I want you to stay put until I return."

"Where are you going?"

"I'm going back to find some answers, but don't worry since you have great security in your building."

Kristina moved closer to him, her body trembled while her perfume reinforced the presence of a woman scared into acting like a young girl. He couldn't blame her, knowing how much of a sheltered life she had lived. He reached around her shoulder to hold her. They would be back at her condo in a few minutes.

After stopping in front of her building, he released her as she reached for his hand. "Thank you."

"Don't mention it. Right now, we need to get you inside."

As soon as she walked by the doorman and entered the care of the building security, he jumped back into the limo and yelled at the driver. "Hurry . . . we need to check this out." As they got closer, he saw maybe ten or twelve police cars ahead of them. "Drop me off here and I can walk." He opened the door and jogged the rest of the way.

A policeman stopped him as he approached a police line being pulled across the sidewalk. "My name's Shawn Davis. I'm the head of security for Lyons International Company, and the one who called this in."

The uniformed officer looked at him with one of those New York policeman attitudes, and as if he didn't believe him until Shawn showed his company issued shield. "Did you see what happened?"

"I was in the crossfire, and I was ducking too much to see anything."

Shawn continued to walk around until he recognized a detective he knew, who was leaning over and checking the broken bottles. "Hello, Shawn, what do you know about this?"

"I was escorting one of my executive's daughters out of the club when I heard these glasses being shattered, I heard at least three." The smell was intent. "What kind of fluid is this?"

"We'll have to test it, but I think it might be muriatic acid, you know, the stuff you use to clean brick with."

Shawn studied the points of impact. "Or attempt to ruin someone's face with shattered glass mixed with acid."

"Did you get any on you or your client?"

"No, I guess we were lucky, or the intent was simply to scare us."

"Whoever did this was long gone before we arrived. I suspect they're in the park somewhere. We have the dogs coming, but I'm sure he has already made it out at some point."

"Is there any chance you can find a finger print on a piece of the glass?"

"Very slim. Do you have any guess why you were being targeted?"

"Nothing that would warrant something like this. Can I get a copy of the report when you're finished?" Shawn handed him one of his cards.

"I'm sure obtaining a copy will not be a problem.

Whoever did this will be hard to catch. You might want to increase your security."

"Yes, I agree."

###

Kristina tried to control her breathing. If she continued at this rate, she knew she would pass out again. Her dad led her to a couch before he grabbed a phone. "Where is Shawn, he doesn't answer."

"He's checking on what happened. He might not be able to answer right now. I'm sure he'll come by here as soon as he knows anything."

Suddenly, her father yelled into the phone."Where are you? I see, come on up. I'll call the guard downstairs."

Kristina breathed easier knowing he was safe. She had never come under an attack like that before. "Let me clean my face before he sees me." She walked off, with her father nodding his head and her mother saying nothing, but holding her hand over her face noticeably in shock at what she had been told.

The cool water on her face erased most of her makeup, but she didn't care if Shawn saw her with none on. She worked to erase all signs of it as her phone vibrated. She had a text message being added. She decided to check them, as she realized she would be changing numbers the next morning. The same message appeared several times. "Until you have an abortion and stop this, count on receiving much of the same you got tonight, bitch."

She dropped the phone and yelled. Moments later her dad and mom came running into her room with Shawn close behind them. Shawn kneeled to retrieve the phone, and tried to hand it to her. "No, I don't want it. Take a look at the message." Her voice trembled in spite of how hard she tried to stay calm.

Shawn read the message. "Damn." He handed it to Lawson.

Lawson turned to Shawn. "Can't we determine whose phone this is?"

"I'm sure it's one of those phones you buy on the street. We can determine where it was purchased, but unless they have a camera installed or the sales clerk remembers the purchaser we'll never know. And . . . I'll assume they were careful in buying it. Kristina needs a new unlisted phone tomorrow morning."

"And there's nothing else you can do?"

"Not totally. I can set up a trace to let me know where the calls are coming from and while he's on the phone be able to know this. If he's close to here, I might be able to use one of the police cameras to spot him, or get there. It's a long shot, but I'll set it up tonight with a friend with the police department."

Kristina turned to Lawson. "This is your fault. No one would have known about this if you hadn't called that stupid board meeting. Now . . . everyone knows."

Her dad snapped back. "Don't blame me for this. It would come out soon enough. You're the one pregnant!"

"And like this is my fault, dad." Kristina lowered herself on to the toilet seat to rest as she felt the tears flowing down her face. Her mother rushed to her side to console her.

While her dad moved closer, and she could feel his presence, he never touched her. Was this only the beginning? She glanced at Shawn. "Please help me find out who's doing this."

"I intend to do exactly that. In the meantime, I can't be with you all of the time, as I have many people in the company to protect, but I think we need to have someone on my staff be with you until this is over. I know you have excellent coverage while inside the building, but he'll be outside and available for any and *all* trips you make outside."

She understood what he was saying as she glanced at her dad. "I understand and appreciate it, but I don't intend to remain inside all of the time. I also hope you can escort me to some of the major events I have to attend."

"I don't think that will be a problem, as long as we don't have a major company function at the same time."

"I understand."

Kristina glanced at the phone. "Someone really wants me to have an abortion."

Her mother spoke for the first time. "I understand someone doesn't want to get caught and be responsible for your baby."

The use of the word baby caught her off guard. That's what she had growing inside of her—a baby. Kristina shut her eyes and shivered. When she opened them, she gazed into Shawn's eyes, which radiated a deep caring for her that she needed. But . . . with her parents nearby, she couldn't say what was on her mind, and in her heart. She could only hope that he could read her eyes as she did his.

Shawn reached out his hand to her dad. "I know your family would like to be alone. You have my word that I'll do everything possible to find out who's responsible, and to keep everyone safe."

"I know you will, and we appreciate all you're doing. I know you'll be interviewing everyone tomorrow. Again . . . keep this as quiet as you can until we decide what to do next."

Kristina glanced at her father. "I'm not sure if I want an abortion, or not. Yes . . . part of me says to do it now, but another part of me says to think about it. I don't know." She glanced back at Shawn, hoping he would support her. A small twinkle in his eyes was all she needed. She needed time to think.

Shawn leaned over toward her. "Again, I'm sorry you have to go through this. I'll be in touch. Please allow me to order you a new phone so that we can have some special features added to it." The two men exchanged a look, indicating they knew what that meant.

When Shawn turned and walked out the door she immediately missed his presence, as she lowered her head and waited for her parents to descend upon her about the abortion.

Chapter 8

Shawn cleared his desk and hid most of the files he had worked on. Today he would be busy all day with over twenty different interviews and conferences. He had scheduled different waiting rooms so no one could compare notes. Each person was told to not discuss the meeting, or even that they had been summoned. He had made this imperative to everyone, but knew some of it would leak out anyway.

A secretary soon announced the first one to arrive, and he was one of the most important. While there were three different bartenders working the celebration cruise and one of them was an older lady, it was Carlos who had worked the main deck where Kristina drank most of the night. His observation would be crucial in discovering who might have slipped something into her drink.

A nervous Carlos walked in. "You wanted to see me, sir?"

Shawn stood for a brief moment. "Please make yourself comfortable and have a seat." Carlos complied, while the focus of his eyes flashed around the room. "As I mentioned to you on the phone this meeting is to be held strictly confidential." Shawn waited for him to nod a yes. "I need you to think back to the night of the celebration on the company yacht about a little over a month ago. You do remember working it, I assume."

"Yes, of course. I was paid well for it."

Shawn decided to get right to the point. "While you were preparing drinks on the cruise, do you remember anyone aboard acting . . . strange?"

Carlos wrinkled his brow. "In which way? Everyone was drinking a lot and having a good time."

"I understand, but did you see anyone acting strange with a drink, or ordering more than they should have?"

Carlos hesitated as the focus of his eyes floated upward. "The only one who I know had way too much to drink was Kristina. I watched Jeff helping her downstairs."

"I heard. How long was he gone with her?"

"Not long . . . maybe ten minutes at the most."

Shawn entered a note which may help to clear Jeff, but he never really considered Jeff to be a prime suspect. "I want you to think. Did you see anyone giving a drink of any kind to Kristina?"

Carlos paused again. "I don't remember her drinking anything but champagne. She generally likes to drink cosmopolitans, but as far as I can remember I never made her one that night."

"I see. How many glasses of champagne do you think she had that night?"

"Since I saw her with one all night, I don't know if she had a new glass, or if she sipped on the same one for a long time. I'm sure the servers will give you a much better answer."

"They'll be in here later. Besides Kristina, who else had a lot to drink?"

"No one person stands out. The only person who doesn't like champagne and prefers his Scotch is Mr. Lyons."

Shawn knew his grandfather preferred Scotch, and this didn't surprise him. "One last thing. Everybody on the cruise is being asked to voluntarily submit a DNA sample."

Carlos eyes widen. "Why?"

"I can't say right now, but if you don't submit one, the police might be asking you to do so later. We would prefer to do this investigation privately, and I hope no one has anything to hide."

"I have done nothing wrong. Am I being accused of something?"

"No, not at all, but we have to ask all onboard to submit in order to narrow our search. Those not submitting a DNA sample will be subject to additional interviews, etc."

"I have nothing to hide. What do I have to do?"

"I'll only need a small hair clipping." He lifted a small pair of scissors and a plastic bag. "You'll sign the seal, and I'll send it off to a lab."

"Let's do it. I have nothing to hide."

"I know you don't, and I'm sorry for this, but I have my orders."

The rest of the day repeated many times with no one noticing anything out of the ordinary. He finally saw Todd's name on the list to come in next. Being an arrogant son of one of the board members, Shawn knew that he would be next to impossible to deal with.

Todd walked in looking like a banker on Wall Street and not like the typical college student that Shawn knew he was. His mannerism was much more polished and under control than he expected. His father must have coached him on how to act, or he was intent on hiding something. "I think it's my time, right?"

"Yes, please come in and have a seat."

Todd looked around. "My father told me what was going on. Let me say I feel sorry for her. She had a lot to drink on the yacht, and I thought that she might be getting herself in trouble." Shawn smiled at the arrogance, and hoped to use it to his favor by allowing him to keep talking. "Dad said you would be collecting DNA samples of every guy on board to see who the guy responsible is, but I can guarantee you that it wasn't me. If I was you, I would concentrate on some of the crew. You never know about those people we use."

"I'll assure you we'll check everyone, and we do appreciate your help." Shawn leaned forward. "How many drinks did you see Kristina have?"

"I'm not sure how many. She had one in her hand the entire evening."

"Did you ever see anything in her hand other than champagne?"

Shawn watched the iris in his eyes expand. "No, I don't think so." Shawn knew he lied or was hiding something.

Shawn lifted the scissor. "I hate to ruin your haircut, but I need only a small sample."

"Not a problem, it will grow back out. Like my father, I wonder why Kristina simply doesn't have an abortion and simply just try to hide this, instead of bringing it to a board meeting accusing everyone of something she brought on herself."

The arrogant bastard; now, the truth was coming out. Like many rich kids and parents they didn't like anything crossing them or reflecting badly on their image.

Shawn wanted to say they suspected she was drugged, but kept the suspicion hidden. "I don't think Kristina wants the world to know. Her father's pushing this toward the board and rightly so. He doesn't want this to turn into a scandal, but handled internally, which is why I'm involved."

"Man, I'm glad I don't have your job."

Shawn studied this guy and wondered what he was hiding, if anything. It was going to be so interesting in seeing the DNA test results. While Kristina now says that she might not have one, he still had to follow his orders and do the best he could. It would be a long day.

Kristina made many calls from her bedroom and listened to one person after another. Her eyes hurt from straining at the computer screen for the last two days. She needed to get ready for her appointment with a gynecologist soon. Since word was circulating, she now needed answers, and she hoped this doctor her mother located would keep his mouth shut. Well, she really thought he would, but the paranoia had already set in. She knew it, even when she fought it as hard as she could.

She had called Shawn personally when the appointment was set. She enjoyed having him looking over her. Many times before she had never paid attention to the bodyguard service, but Shawn was different. She finished checking her outfit and walked out to see her mother, who was waiting on her.

"You look good." Her mother looked more apprehensive than she would have assumed. The last few days had impacted her and lowered her energy and arrogance, making her much more reserved than normal. Her mother hated bad publicity, and she would do almost anything to squash it.

"Mom, you look tired."

"It has been an exhausting few days. I hope this visit will be fruitful."

"Do you mean as far as convincing me to have an abortion?"

"I want you to decide what you do. I'll support you either way, but I need to make plans based on what you want."

Kristina could see the wheels turning. Was her mother planning on shipping her off, say to Europe, for an extended stay to have a baby? She studied her mother closer. Surely not.

The doorman buzzed them. "Mrs. Sutherland, your ride's here."

"Thank you, we'll be down in a few moments." She turned to her daughter. "I want to protect you, but I'm having a hard time deciding what is the best way to do that."

"Mom, you know I'm a grown woman, and I can make some decisions on my own."

"Yes, but we have always been here for you."

The truth hurt, but her mother was right; her parents had done everything for her. While it was time to make some changes, she first she needed to get past this. "Thanks, but just don't push me right now."

Her mother only glared at her as they headed downstairs.

###

While Shawn checked out the sidewalk and

surveyed the street activity, he had no plans on being blindsided again. No one knew about this trip, and he hoped he would quickly have everyone inside the limo. He had already visited the doctor's office and planned his entry.

When he saw the two women walking pass the doorman, he hurried to escort them inside the limo, her mother first. He did notice a sly smile when he helped Kristina inside, which he felt obliged to return.

Once inside, he turned to them. "We'll be there in a few minutes, since it's not far. We'll be going down a hallway they use for deliveries."

While the mother ignored his presence, Kristina openly studied him. It felt weird, as he looked straight ahead to avoid eye contact. When the limo came to a stop, he jumped out to check the entrance. After the driver joined him, they nodded an all clear.

On the way in, Barbara walked ahead of him as Kristina accepted an arm. He knew she wasn't so far along as to needing any help, but he sensed she needed this more in the way of a mental support.

After making it along a hallway, they rode an elevator to the doctor's floor, where the mother turned to him. "I'm not sure how long we'll be. Make yourself comfortable and I'll let you know when we're done." He knew it was her way of saying this was as far as he would be allowed. This was fine by him. He searched for a place to sit and wait.

###

Kristina walked slowly toward the outer office as a nurse quickly met them. "Ms. Sutherland?"

"Yes."

"Please come on back with me. The doctor's

waiting on you."

Since her mother acted like she was going back with her, Kristina stopped and glanced at her. "I think I'll be fine on my own."

The nurse picked up on the conversation. "You can stay here in the inner waiting room if you wish."

"Yes, I think that would be better than going outside and being spotted."

Kristina ignored her mother and followed the nurse, who quickly checked her blood pressure and her weight while asking a few questions. However . . . her thoughts remained on Shawn. She hadn't had a chance to talk to him for several days, and she wanted to know what he might have discovered.

Perhaps because he was paying more attention to her than the other guards, she felt an undeniable attraction toward him. Strange, but she couldn't forget his physical shape, his face, or even his personality, which had never changed for the worse so far. He had an inner confidence that wasn't faked or pretentious, as so many other people around her were so often.

Lost in her thoughts, she didn't realize the nurse had left her alone. Words Shawn had used to describe how he wouldn't be here if his mother had optioned for an abortion haunted her. She was carrying a baby inside her. This would be someone who depended on her, and something she had never experienced before. It was the photos she couldn't erase from her mind. She should've never gone to those sites.

The doctor entered, wearing his white coat and a pleasant smile. "Hello. How are you today?"

"I'm not sure. As you probably know from the appointment, and the information I had to fill out, I'm pregnant."

The doctor settled into a small seat in front of her. "I see you have taken a home test."

"And I went to a clinic to have it confirmed. I assume you want to do it again."

"No, I think we can believe you're pregnant. " He looked over the file. "I see that you're single. Has the father been notified?"

"I'm not sure who the father is."

The doctor showed no emotions. "I see. Well . . . based on your last known period, it looks like you have around seven months to go. Do you have someone who can help you along?"

"Yes, I live with my parents." At twenty-five she knew this sounded bad, but it was the truth, and they did provide everything she needed. Well, almost everything.

"It appears that you're healthy, so you shouldn't have any problems with delivery. We'll set you up with a schedule to follow, and I'll be with you all of the way."

"Since I don't know who the father is, I might be considering an abortion. This is one of the things I wanted to talk to you about."

The doctor adjusted his seat, acting like he was surprised. "I know it's a normal reaction to think of such, but usually more so when we have a case of rape, etc."

"You know, I cannot rule it out. I had a night I don't remember much of."

The doctor's interest intensified. "Have you reported this to the police?"

"I don't have anything really to report. I have

someone doing some investigations, and I really can't go into all of the details now." She sobbed two times, but forced herself to focus.

"I understand now. After this length of time I doubt if your body has any chemicals remaining, but we can test just in case."

"I would appreciate it."

"Let me ask you a few questions. When you say you don't remember anything, do you think you were unconscious, or simply paralyzed and unable to move?"

"I don't remember anything at all."

"I see. Do you have any nightmares about what happened?"

"No, other than nightmares about what I'm facing."

"I guess that's one silver lining in all of this. In such a case we need to do some tests to make sure the baby itself is healthy."

"In the investigations they're doing, they're collecting DNA samples. When will I be able to have a DNA test to determine who the baby's father is?"

"All we need is a sample of the baby's body fluid to establish the DNA. We should be able to obtain it with no problems soon."

"Good, I think I want to wait until we receive the DNA test from the others. Also . . . I'm not sure which way I want to go."

"It's a difficult decision, I know. This is why I asked if you have a good support group around you. A baby can be a life changing experience. I have four girls at home, and I can attest to how great they make my life." He pointed to a picture on the wall. "This is my family."

Thoughts of her holding a baby ushered in a small confusing note. Was she ready to be a mother? "I need to know about an abortion. What's involved, and is it painful?"

"It's not painful at all. We can use an abortion pill which induces your period by blocking your pregnancy hormones. This causes the menstrual lines to separate from the uterus. We use a second medication to cause the uterus to contract, which in turn expels the menstrual lining, completing the abortion. This is the preferred method in an early abortion. It can all be handled in under one hour."

"I see."

"I don't perform them here, but I can line one up for you."

"Why don't you perform them?"

"Of all of the doctors you could have picked, I'm the one who thinks that all life is precious, but it's not my right to impose my beliefs on you. I'll simply not perform them personally."

"So, you think they're wrong."

"It's my opinion, but like I said, every woman has to make up her own mind. If you decide to have the baby, I'll help you every step of the way." She watched him smile at the photo of his girls.

"I think you've answered some questions for me. I'm confused. I need some time to think."

"That's understandable, but be careful, since New York City's known to be the abortion capital of the world. The culture here is full of easy abortions."

"Thanks, I'll let you know what I decide."

Chapter 9

After Shawn escorted Kristina and her mother from the limo, he stopped to say goodbye while Kristina looked at her mother. "I want Shawn to come up for a minute. I would like to know what he had discovered so far in his investigations."

Shawn glanced at the limo. "Let me tell the driver to go on." Shawn hoped to have all of the interviews completed and in a nice neat report before he had to disclose what he suspected. Since the DNA would be the final convincing evidence, he felt sure that was what the doctor visit was all about.

As they walked by the company security guard who waved at Shawn, it felt good to know his people were safe at night. After making it into their place, her mother led them to a small office. "I also would like to know what you've discovered."

"First let me say that I'm still interviewing. No one has seen anything which helps. I have the DNA samples from all of the men on the list I needed. These have all been submitted, and the results should be back in about a week."

"Why so long?"

"That's what it takes. How long will it take for you to get your DNA results back from the doctor you visited today?"

Kristina spoke. "I didn't allow him to take DNA today. I think it's too early."

"In such a case, we might not know who the

attacker is until your tests are completed."

"My dad's not going to like this." Kristina rubbed her stomach. Since the baby couldn't be causing her any major problems this early, Shawn knew she had to be thinking about it and thinking about what the doctor had told her.

Kristina looked at her mother. "They want to do some tests to make sure the baby's fine. By not knowing who the father is, the doctor simply wants to play it safe."

Her mother stared first at Kristina, and then at him, placing him in an awkward position before she asked, "Kristina, are you thinking of having this baby?"

"I really can't see myself as a mother, but I also know I'm carrying some illegitimate baby in my stomach. However, I don't like everyone telling me what to do. I've had several friends who have had abortions, but I never thought I would be put in such a position."

Shawn smiled, hoping his words had gotten through to her. "I know this is hard for you, and I wish I had more information for you. If you decide to keep this baby, I'm sure you'll be a great mother."

Kristina smiled for the first time today. "Thanks."

Her mother apparently didn't like the way the conversation was going, as she turned to Shawn. "I hope you keep digging. After this attempt on Kristina's life, I'm sure whoever did this has no intentions of being a father or taking responsibility."

"Whenever we have the DNA test, we'll have no problem determining who it is. And . . . in such a case, I'm sure he'll be receiving some jail time." Shawn studied Kristina's hair as she leaned over. She looked good, too good. He had to remember who she was—a girl totally unavailable for someone like him.

Kristina locked eyes with him. "Thank you for everything. Please let me know of anything you find out."

"I will. Goodnight for now." Shawn turned and left, knowing he would be seeing much more of her over the next seven months.

Chapter 10

Shawn finished another file and added it to the stack on his desk. Nothing pointed to one specific person. His best guess would be one of the preppy sons, but he had no proof. Except for the older men on the cruise, he had DNA samples from everyone. As soon as Kristina supplied the DNA for the baby, he would know for sure.

His phone rang. "Shawn."

"Yes, this is Lawson. We're having a small meeting upstairs, and I want you to bring us up to date on what you've learned about Kristina's rapist. Come on up, we're waiting on you."

He knew they wanted answers, but he had none. He retrieved a summary file and a note pad. Lawson wanted justice and he could not blame him, but at the same time his actions were causing problems. This story would hit the main media if he kept at it.

He decided to hike the stairs instead and enjoy the workout. After entering the executive floor, he knew he could find Lawson easily, but surprisingly a secretary directed him to his grandfather's office. Brent Lyon smiled at him as he entered and motioned to a chair at a conference table where Lawson was sitting.

As instructed, he moved into a seat and watched his grandfather take his before he started. "I've been working on this hard, but I have no proof of who's the person responsible. It'll all come down to the DNA test."

Brent looked at Lawson. "My old friend. I know this is terrible, and how you must feel. We both know once the attacker is discovered a long and painful trial will take place. I would hate to see my daughter pulled though such an ordeal. A quick abortion and privacy might do more for you and your family than getting your revenge."

Lawson turned toward Shawn. "Brent's words make sense, but I still want to know the truth." He paused. "And Kristina's leaning more and more toward keeping the baby."

Brent tightened his fist as he focused on him. "I've heard that you have encouraged Lawson's daughter to *not have* an abortion."

"She asked my opinion, and I gave it." *Watch it old man, there's a limit to what I will put up with.* He locked eyes with his grandfather as he entered a battle of wills. Shawn knew he would be back to see his grandfather later when Lawson wasn't around.

"I think the purpose of this meeting is to let you know you need to keep your opinions to yourself. Is that understood?"

"Yes, sir." That was for now. He wouldn't be working here too much longer. This sealed his future. Yes, he could and would make it on his own. He stood to leave. "Is there anything else?"

Lawson stood. "Please wait a minute. I know you're working hard on this, and I never had a chance to thank you for protecting my daughter the other night from the bottle attack in front of the Manhattan Club." He leaned closer toward Brent. "We also have some differences of opinion, but my daughter feels safe with you, and I know this will only get nastier. I want you to still escort her when you can. I know you have other duties, but when you can, work it out. As a personal favor for me, I plan to make it worth your while, with a large bonus."

Brent appeared to not like the bonus part. "If he insists on causing problems, he might be looking for a new job."

"I don't think so. What's your problem, Brent?"

Brent's attitude appeared to change as Lawson raised his tone. Brent lowered his voice to respond, "I'm sorry. This has been a strain on all of us. We'll get through it."

Lawson rubbed his eyes. "That . . . it has been. I only have the one daughter."

Chapter 11

As the maid answered another call, Kristina shook her head. She had enough and didn't want to speak with anyone. One girlfriend after another had called her, and even a radio station reporter had tried to talk to her. *Where is my mother?*

Kristina glanced at the maid. "Don't answer the phone anymore. Let the damn answer machine take it!"

Who let the word out? A sickening panic crept over her, since she knew this would only be the beginning. One of the reporters had actually used the word, rape.

"I'm going out on the patio to think for a minute." After walking out to the balcony and overlooking the city, she studied the fading sunlight and the beginning of the night life, where the office lights indicated just how many people were working late.

Taxi horns and sirens echoed off various buildings, as the rising waves of food smells flooded the air from the restaurants below. She used to love to walk the streets when she was younger. Funny, she felt safe earlier. That was before her father made a name for himself in the company and he had become so famous. Adding the gaming section to the company changed everything.

The glass behind her cracked as a loud popping sound followed it. As she swirled to see the glass door behind her, it crashed to the floor. She stumbled backwards and fell as another pop sent a hole thought the adjacent door. Bullets! Someone was shooting at her. She hit the tile floor and screamed.

A maid quickly appeared, yelling for her. "Oh my god, what is it?"

"Get down! We're being shot at." The maid immediately disappeared, but Kristina had no way to move without being exposed. She slipped her hand into her pocket to retrieve her phone, where she quickly dialed 911. "I need help. Someone's shooting at me!"

"Seek cover immediately; we'll be there in a few minutes. We have your address. Do you see the attacker?"

"No, listen I'll be back in a minute. I need to call security downstairs." She intended to speed dial the company guard, but reached Shawn.

"How are you, Kristina?"

"Shawn, I have someone firing at me on the patio outside our condo."

"What?" Get inside and out of sight; I'm on the way."

"I can't get inside. I'm on the ground, hiding behind a planter."

"I'm five blocks away, but will be there in a few minutes. Stay down."

While the seconds seemed like hours, she heard no more shots, but knew bullets had to be what shattered the glass. She wanted to look over the side, but she was too scared to move. Was it a random shooting or was she actually targeted?

The maid yelled from around the corner, "Security will be here in a minute. They're on the way up now!"

"Good, you stay down also."

She heard movement as several men rushed into the room behind the glass shattered everywhere. One of them rushed over and kneeled beside her. She suddenly recognized Shawn, who held a hand on top of her head. "Stay down." Damn, he must have run hard.

She watched him peek over the top of the wall for several minutes before lowering back down to her. "I can see nothing. We're going to make a dash for it. I'll shield you."

He gave her no choice, as he lifted her and ran with her inside the room. He didn't stop until he entered the main living area. Many more men rushed by her and out onto the roof top balcony, taking up positions. "Are you okay?"

"Yes, but scared shitless."

"I understand, but you're safe now."

A police officer kneeled closer to her. "Could you tell where the shots came from?"

"No, the only sound I heard was the glass shattering."

"What about any flash of light?"

"No, nothing."

"I understand. We have a helicopter soon in the air to check out all of the roof tops around here, but it will take some time."

"Is this your boyfriend?"

The question caught her off guard, but considering how he was holding her she could see how the officer might be confused. "No, this is my bodyguard."

Shawn reached for his badge. "I'm head of security for the Lyon International. Kristina's the daughter of one of the board members."

The officer glanced around and lowered his voice. "Do you have any idea who's behind this sniper attack?"

"No, but I might have a clue. My company's doing an investigation right now. There's nothing I can report now, but I will as soon as it's completed. Did you find the bullets?"

"We located one hole in the wall and have a team coming who will hunt for the second one. Damn, this condo has a lot of glass windows."

"Yes, but if you have a million dollar view, you would want to enjoy it."

The officer leaned over to speak to Kristina. "Who lives here with you?"

"I live with my parents, but we have four staff workers who come and go all day."

"Let me ask you this. Do you think the sniper was targeting you or your parents?"

"I don't know who would want to do this." She lowered her head and cried. A soothing arm around her shoulder felt so reassuring, as she hugged Shawn's back and wanted to vanish inside his security.

The office shook his head. "I know this is a bad time, but I'll have more questions later."

One of the maids walked in. "I heard from your parents, and they'll be here shortly."

Shawn whispered in her ear. "I think I need to get you to your bed and let you rest for a minute."

She felt too scared and uptight to lie on her bed, that is, unless he wanted to lie beside her. She didn't want to venture away from him. Her fingers wrapped around a piece of his shirt, holding on tightly. "Stay with me, I don't want to be alone."

"Don't worry. I'm here, and your parents will be here soon."

The officer looked at Shawn. "Until we secure this area and find out who is doing this, it might be good for them to stay somewhere else."

"Yes, I have considered this. I'm sure something can be worked out when her parents get here."

Kristina listened to the words and wondered where she could be safe. She knew of only one place.

Shawn shifted his weight in the oversized chair while staring at the closed door to Lawson's home office. An occasional loud shout penetrated the silence. Lawson had ordered additional security for the building, and Shawn had posted one guy permanently outside. But instead of being able to do his job, he was told to wait outside.

The door swung open exposing Lawson's deep red face. "Come on in."

Shawn inhaled a deep breath and stood. Kristina sat next to her mother who had wrapped her arms around her, but had her head hung. This was one of those family moments even the rich have to face. *Why am I being asked to attend?*

Lawson wasted no time in getting the meeting under way. "This is the second time someone has tried to hurt, or kill my daughter. It's your job to protect us."

"Yes, sir, it is. We'll have to take some extreme measures."

"Agreed. The police say my home, my home, is not safe!"

"It does have a lot of glass windows, sir."

"I'm having them replaced with bulletproof windows. The cost will be outrageous, but I've no choice. I do have another place to go until it's completed, but Kristina doesn't want to go there."

Kristina chin quivered. "I need to go somewhere no one will look for me until you find out who's after me. We all know it has to be someone who drugged me. I have no choice now but to have the DNA test completed as soon as possible."

"I agree. Until this is over, we need to check you in somewhere very secure and safe."

Lawson snorted, as the anger escaped his control. "She has in her mind a place she wants to go, and she will not tell me or anyone."

"Really, why is that?"

Kristina turned toward him. "I trust no one now, except you. You'll be the only one who'll know where I am. I don't want word of this to get out again." She glared at her father, as Shawn knew she blamed him for disclosing she was pregnant in the first place.

Shawn turned to Lawson for advice. "Sir, I'm willing to do whatever you want."

"I appear to have no choice. She's a grown woman now, and she sure doesn't need to go off totally on her own. I'll push the doctor to return the DNA results as fast as possible."

Shawn faced Kristina. "I still need to know where you're thinking of staying, so that I can check it out and provide the proper security."

Kristina pulled away from her mother. "I want to leave later tonight, and I'll tell you as soon as we're alone. I can pack what I need in a few hours." As

Shawn and Lawson exchanged a stare, Kristina continued, "If I know you two talk, I'll leave on my own. I hope this is clear."

Kristina had a way of placing him in a bad situation. Lawson wouldn't like it, but still he knew that Lawson realized it wasn't his fault as Lawson spoke to Kristina, "I think you're being ridiculous."

"I think you and your pride is what has caused me to do this, dad, so don't say a word."

Lawson walked closer, as Barbara bit her lip before she added, "In this case I think your daughter's right. You should not have taken it to the board until we know more about what happened."

"Yes, but we now have the DNA samples, which will tell us who did this!"

"Dad, don't you realize my life will be on public display forever if this goes to trial. I don't want that."

Lawson looked like a man who was outnumbered and pushed to the limits. "Anyway, this will only be for a few days. The contractors will be here tomorrow to start changing out the windows." He turned to Shawn. "She's in your hands." Lawson reached for his wife's hand and pulled her behind him as they left the room.

Shawn waited on Kristina to tell him where he would be taking her, but instead, she hung her head in silence. He knew she had gone through a lot, as he walked over to her and kneeled next to her. "I'm glad you're safe."

"Yeah, like someone just tried to kill me."

"I had a few minutes to analyze the bullet hole, and from the angle the bullet entered from the glass door I don't think they wanted to kill you, but only scare you."

"They sure the hell did that."

"My guess from everything is that someone wants to stop you from having the DNA test and opt for an abortion."

"But who?"

"I think we'll know as soon as the DNA results come back. I do need to know where I'm taking you."

"I'll tell you soon. For now arrange for a limo to take me to your place where we can get your car."

"My car?"

"Yes. I don't even want the driver to know where I'm staying. You'll be the only one."

Shawn realized she had given this some thought. "Depending on where this is, I might have to arrange for additional security."

"Trust me, it will not be necessary. Now, if you'll excuse me, I need to pack."

###

Kristina's head felt light, but she needed to take control. Someone had violated her, and had his way with her, impregnating her no less. Her own dad had as much as broadcasted it to the world. She knew her world was collapsing and was now needing constant monitoring, since her life had come under attack twice. Enough was enough. Shawn was the only one who could help her and give her time to think about what she needed to do.

They waited until late that night to leave. Shawn had it planned to escort her to the waiting limo without being seen. Minutes later, they sped off toward his place, where the driver stood guard as they moved her luggage to his car. Shawn waved for the driver to leave first.

Shawn leaned over to her. "Okay, I need to know where we're going."

"The lights in the park look great this time of year." She needed a few minutes to make sure the driver had disappeared, and for her to get her nerves up on what she had planned.

"We're not going through the park."

"No, but around it. It'll only take a minute." She had driven in a normal sized car only a few times, and the sights were so much different with all of the windows around her.

After making the circle and arriving back on Fifth and Park, she offered new directions at each intersection. "There, that's where we need to go."

"This is back where we started."

"I know. Pull in quickly so we'll not be seen."

While he felt confused, he complied. "You need to let me know what's going on."

"I cannot think of anywhere more secure than this place. No one will look here, ever."

"You saw my place once. It's not like what you're used to. And . . . I only have one large room."

"I think we can manage for a few days. Your place is built like Fort Knox."

"Your father would kill me."

"He'll never know. Do you know of any place better?"

She had him and appeared to know it. "Okay, since it will be only for a few days."

Chapter 12

Shawn stretched and rubbed his shoulder. Yes, he had slept on his couch before. He reached over to the floor and scratched Lucy's head. At least she didn't complain about sleeping on the floor. He needed to do his morning exercises, but he certainly didn't think he should wake his new guest this early.

He started slow as he stretched his muscles and allowed the flow of energy to increase. First he had to release the bad and cleanse his body. After a day like yesterday, it would take some time before he could clear his mind.

As he turned to face the morning light floating through the eastern window, he glanced at his bed. All he saw was a large lump where he normally slept, with one exception; Kristina had slipped one leg out from under his bedcover. Her bare leg appeared to glow in the early morning light, as the fold in the cover was barely high enough to cover everything else. For a second, he wondered if she was wearing panties. He had to turn away. A relationship with her would run his career forever.

He started his routine with a pace he normally couldn't maintain. His mind couldn't erase the sights of a beautiful woman in his bedroom. This was crazy.

He grabbed the leash and whistled for Lucy. "Come on girl, it's time for a run."

###

While she had pretended to be asleep, Kristina

watched Shawn work out. His raw well-toned muscles had excited her. He looked good—no, he looked fantastic.

She would dress while he was gone. He didn't lie about his place providing only the basic necessities. Still, she felt secure in Shawn's place. Maybe it was the fact that no one would bother her and she would have no staff looking over her shoulder, or schedules for her to keep. While only a few blocks away, she felt like she was in a different world.

She laughed at his closet—a rod stretched between two posts. How could anyone live as open as this? She started to go to one of the windows and look out, but decided against it. How far did Shawn run? Running outside would be interesting and different from the gym she normally went to.

She suddenly felt like snooping, but felt tense in doing so. What if she had him all wrong and he wasn't the gentleman he had appeared to be? She really didn't know much about it. Maybe she should find out something about him. She quickly slipped into some leisure clothes she had brought with her.

His belongings were simple. He had very few pictures on a wall, but on one wall he had many books neatly assigned, and almost all of them were on martial arts. In one corner of the flat, she noticed a box where inside she examined many trophies. All of them were martial arts related.

She went through these many times, until she heard noises on the stairways. Lucy burst through the door first and headed straight for her which startled her, making her stumble backwards. Thinking she was going to be attacked, she raised her hands to her face, but Lucy walked in front of her and cocked her head to one side while waited on her to move.

Shawn walked in next. "Lucy, be nice."

Embarrassed, Kristina reached over and rubbed Lucy's head. "I'm not used to dogs."

"They say dogs are a man's best friend, and true friend will stand beside you, no matter what."

"Yes, I've heard that."

"Lucy appears to like you, Kristina."

Looking around the room, she spotted Lucy's feed bowl. "Is it alright if I feed her?"

"I think she would love the attention, but don't spoil her, she only gets so much exercise a day. I also give her a treat every morning after our run. By the way, I brought you something." He reached for a small package he had with him. "I don't know if you like bagels or not, so I purchased several different items for you."

"Everyone in New York loves bagels." She glanced at the small kitchen area. "Do you cook much here?"

"Not really. It's easier to stop on the street. You would probably not like the kind of food I eat." He pointed to the refrigerator.

She couldn't resist and walked toward it. "May I?" Since he didn't respond, she thought she had permission and opened the door. "Oh, my gosh."

"I try to eat lots of raw vegetables and fruits."

"You know, I've never tried to cook a meal on my own before. Do you think we could try it?"

"Sure, we have to eat. What are you thinking of trying?"

"I don't know. I'll let you know."

"Okay, but for now we need to see about getting the DNA sample, so we can find a match with the ones we've collected."

"I know. I'll call the doctor and set it up for this afternoon. It'll be your responsibility to get me in and out, as usual, without being seen."

"I can manage that. I do have to go to the office for a while, but I'll leave Lucy with you, and you can call me if you have any reason to become alarmed."

"I'll be fine. You know to say nothing, and trust me, my father will be asking."

"I know. I'll not be too long, but I do have to coordinate my staff on their duties as well."

"Is it okay if I use your computer to see how to cook something?"

"Sure." He walked over to a small table and added a password. "I'll be back soon."

"I'll call you soon with a shopping list for tonight. We can try cooking after we see the doctor." A release in tension flowed over her as she anticipated a night of relaxing without being so uptight. While this wasn't what she was used to, it was perfect for what she needed now. It felt great to be hiding out and be off public display. She looked forward to spending time with Shawn. Now if she could only get him to relax and have some fun tonight.

###

As soon as Shawn walked into his office, he saw a note from Lawson to come see him, but he had expected such and was prepared. He stopped only long enough to cover some upcoming events. The main shift would be the same as the previous for the corporate headquarters. Other than the problem with

Kristina, he had no major demands on his time.

He walked into Lawson's office and closed the door behind him. "I think you wanted to see me."

He smiled and walked over to him, extending him his hand. "I want to apologize if I came across as too over protective of my daughter."

"Not a problem and understandable."

"I just got off the phone with the police. Because of the angle of the bullet and how it could have deflected, it will be hard to determine where it was fired. There could be over thirty main roof tops with a clear view. The bullet was from a 30-06. Do you know of such?"

"Yes, they are used for hunting mainly, and the kind of gun many people might have in their closet who enjoy hunting trips."

"Yes, but not in New York City."

"That kind of gun makes one hell of a sound when it's fired."

"Kristina said she heard nothing. What do you think?"

"I'll have to check to see if they make a silencer for it. If so, we might be looking at a professional, rather than an individual shooter."

"I don't like the sounds of this. How long will it be until we know who the rapist is?"

"I'm taking Kristina to the doctor today to obtain the DNA samples. It will be rushed as fast as possible. When we have the evidence, you'll have to decide what to do with it."

"Yes, please don't disclose anything until you talk to me first. My daughter's already mad enough at me for my actions. By the way, I assume you have her somewhere safe."

"Yes, it's somewhere that she decided on." Shawn knew he wanted to know where she was. "She'll be safe."

"I would like to believe you. You know, I'll not tell anyone if you told me."

"Still, if word gets out I did, she'll never trust me or you again. At this time, that might be a bad decision."

"Okay, I hate to disagree with you, but you have a point. Please tell her I love her and I want her to be safe."

"I can do that, and I don't think she doubts that in any way, sir."

Lawson smiled. "It's okay to drop the *sir*. Do you have any news on the guy who threw the bottles the other night?"

"No, but I would bet it's someone paid to do so. I think their intent was to scare, not injure. Someone, I think, really wants this to go away, and especially for her to have an abortion."

Lawson glanced at the door. "Brent left here a few minutes ago and also asked why I couldn't talk her into having one."

Shawn felt the anger rise, and his face burning with the rush of blood. Yes, he knew why. This must be reminding him of his daughter he had tried to talk into an abortion many years ago, the abortion that would have ended his life.

"Do me one more favor. Let me know how the doctor visit goes okay." Lawson turned toward the window and continued without looking at him. "I keep thinking about Kristina, and what it would be like to have a grandson. If she decides to go through with this, I'll have to support her."

It was a crack in his armor, but a nice one. Perhaps it would all work out after all. "I'm sure you'll have a great grandson, or, you know, granddaughter."

Shawn watched Lawson smile and bite his lip. This must be where Kristina learned this habit. "I'll call you later."

Lawson only nodded as he left.

Chapter 13

Shawn pulled into his parking place inside the small garage leading to a loading dock. From this part of the building workers in the past could load a truck at night in safety and deliver the goods the next day. He never knew exactly what they sold, but it must have been a thriving business at one time. Now, it was totally abandoned.

He reached in the back and lifted the bags of groceries he had purchased. A large home cooked meal would be nice, and he had also prepared for the worst, especially if she had never cooked before. He selected items which would be too hard to completely ruin, like steak and potatoes, and raw vegetables that only needed cutting.

It might only be for tonight, but having a beautiful woman in his place to spend time with definitely lifted his sprits. He envisioned the bottle of wine he had purchased. To him a major purchase at $40, but he felt sure nothing special to her. Still, he would enjoy it.

Lucy rushed to greet him as he walked in. He saw Kristina nowhere. "Kristina."

A voice on the other side of the bathroom responded. "I'm in here. Give me a minute."

Shawn smiled as he rubbed Lucy's head. "So how was your morning?" With Lucy wagging her tail, he knew she had been pampered well. He studied the room and his pull-down bed replaced in an upright position, something he didn't normally do since he used the bed as an extra couch while he was there.

Kristina emerged as he placed the last of the food away. She had selected a business type suit like she was going for an interview on Wall Street, not simply to a doctor's office for a quick procedure. "You look good."

"Thanks. I hope you can get me in and out without being noticed, but just in case I wanted to be prepared."

Shawn glanced at the four inch heels. They would make it impossible to run for even a short distance if they had to. "I hope we can find something to cover you as much as possible. That would help a lot."

"I have a scarf and a coat I can raise the collar on."

"It'll have to do." Shawn pointed to the refrigerator. "I picked up a few things for tonight, but if you need to me to get anything else just let me know."

He watched Kristina smile as she glanced to the computer. "I've been doing some research. I have a list on the desk we'll need."

Shawn went to the computer and retrieved the list. "Humm, I'll need to go back out again. Are you sure you want to try this?"

"Yes, why not? It will be fun."

Shawn looked back over the list. The meal would cost a lot. He smiled as he wondered how he could fit this into his expense report. "I'll go back out after we see the doctor."

"I saw that smile; you don't think I can cook it, do you?"

"No, that's not why I smiled. I was thinking where I can find the items on your list." He hoped the quick response helped him to save face.

"I'll admit this is a new experience for me, but I expect you to help me."

"That will be interesting. The hardest thing I ever tried to cook was a pizza."

"A pizza?"

"Well yes, but from scratch. It's not as easy as you might think."

"I don't guess you get many deliveries here, do you?"

"No, but around here I can always run out and get some Chinese."

"I appreciate the vote of confidence."

As Shawn imagined the night, he realized he had no candles, and if it would be appropriate to use them if he did. Enjoying a nice dinner was one thing, but a romantic diner was a different story. Perhaps the nice wine would be wrong.

While he was thinking and rereading the list, she moved closer to him. "I didn't add a wine to the list, but we need some kind of robust red I think."

"You know being pregnant . . . you don't need to drink too much."

"I don't think one or two glasses will hurt anything." Kristina patted her stomach. "From what I have read, the baby will not be even visible to the naked eye for another month."

Shawn had a new sense of baby as they talked. He had known for a long time that when and if he ever became a dad, he would work to be the best dad ever, something he'd never had. He also realized that Kristina had a lot to learn also about taking care of her baby. "Well, I'm sure you want to do the best for your baby."

Kristina's eyes rolled upward for a minute. "I think we had this conversation earlier, and I know you think all women should have their babies—regardless."

"I have my reasons and you know it, but you'll have to make your own decision."

"Normally this would be a no brainer for me, but with everyone pushing me to have one I think the rebel in me is coming out. Also I'm having these strange feelings, since your opinions and arguments make sense."

Shawn leaned closer. "I would say I'm proud of you, but I'm not sure my opinion would mean a lot to you."

"Actually, it would." Shawn felt her arm snaking around his back to return his hug. With her body pressed firmly against his, he realized she was more woman than he considered earlier.

After changing his focus from the list of items he needed to buy, he studied her face from inches away now. While her makeup looked good, she didn't need it. Her face looked flawless. Her soft, luscious eyelashes fluttered with ease below a dark brow which had been plucked into a neat enhancing line. The bluish eye shadow highlighted her bright crystal blue eyes. If eyes were the entrance into a soul, he stood at the doorsteps, hesitating, waiting for the strength to walk in.

As she inched closer, he could feel her breath on his face. He had to stop this. With the hardest decision he had ever made, he hugged her tighter but raised his head, taking it out of range of an improper kiss.

He felt her rest her head against his shoulder for a

second before lifting her own head. "I guess we need to go."

###

Kristina listened to Shawn make a call for one of his guards from work to join him at the hospital where the doctor worked. As he pulled his car into a side street by a rear entrance, she noticed a guard standing by the back door giving a small wave. Shawn leaned toward her. "We need to hurry."

While she hated dodging in and out of the hospital, it did have a certain element of excitement to it. She danced on the top of her toes to avoid extra pressure on her heels as she half ran to the back door. She reached for and received Shawn's hand, firmly fitting her smaller hand inside his. The connection felt so natural, as if she had made this connection for a long time, and not for the first time.

After making it to the entrance to the doctor's office, she still held to his hand until she noticed the guard staring at it. She dropped Shawn's hand and straightened her suit. "I think I can take it from here."

Shawn pointed to a row of chairs. "We'll be here if you need us."

While walking through the door, she realized how all alone she was. Yes, she knew how inappropriate it would be for Shawn to be with her inside, but she would have loved for him to be there with her at this moment.

A nurse greeted her in seconds and ushered her back to an examination room. "He'll be with you in a few minutes. Let's get you stats out of the way." Much like a robot, Kristina went through the procedures. She had questions for the doctor, but making a decision on the baby would not be made today. She needed more time.

The doctor soon joined her with a stern look on his face. "How are you today?"

"I'm fine, I guess, but I'm just nervous about what all is going on."

"I received a call this morning from someone who refused to identify himself. I don't like being threatened."

"What do you mean?"

"I was told to make sure I talked you into an abortion today, or else."

"Or else—what?"

"I don't know. They hung up."

"Oh shit. I have the head of security with the company with me as my bodyguard today. I'm sure he'll want to talk to you."

"Someone doesn't want you to have this baby. I really need to report this to the police."

"Yeah, we both know why."

"We'll try to get a DNA on the baby today, but it's not going to be easy. It's still too early to be totally accurate. There simply isn't much embryo fluid to access."

"I think we need to try. The sooner we know who the father is, the better." Kristina closed her eyes and allowed her mind to fall in a trance like state.

"Let me say I don't take threats very well, and I admire you for at least considering keeping the baby. You know you'll have my support if you do."

"Thanks."

Chapter 14

Shawn returned to his place as he analyzed all of the facts, but he still drew blanks as he couldn't determine which guy was responsible for raping, and then attempting to stop Kristina from pursuing who he is. First the phone calls and text messages well planned to not be traced, next the bottles thrown as a warning by someone who escaped easily into Central Park, and finally the shots fired at a glass door beside her, but probably far enough way to insure she wasn't killed. And now, of all things, this threat on the life of the doctor who she was seeing added to the mystery.

While he had to report to the board of directors and Kristina's father, he knew information was leaking back to whoever was responsible. He needed to have a serious talk with Lawson for the sake of his daughter.

Kristina emerged from his bathroom dressed in more casual clothing. "Did you get everything from the store?"

"Yes, this will be interesting watching you."

"Hey, we're in this together."

After considering what she had been through, Shawn noticed a resilience that he admired. Keeping her smiling and comfortable would go a long way in making it through the next few days. As soon as the DNA came back and the rapist was identified, this would all be over for him.

Cutting the vegetables wasn't hard, but preparing the meat was another thing. Cutting pockets in the chicken to place the blue cheese and ham proved to be a challenge. He knew without properly tying it up, the cheese would ooze out and burn while in the oven.

Still, an hour later, they enjoyed burnt meat with undercooked vegetables. At least the wine tasted good. As the candle light casted a dim light on the meal hardly eaten by either, but contained the memories of a fun night, he knew he would remember it for a long time.

Shawn retrieved his glass and finished the last of the first glass of wine, while he noticed she had already finished her own. "Here let me pour you some more."

"I'm surprised you knew how to select such a great bottle of wine."

"Thanks." The compliment made him feel good, but the truth was he had asked for advice, since he knew very little about wines. His discipline to his martial arts study and life style dictated a healthier diet.

"I think some cooking classes would be good. What do you think?"

"If you enjoy it, why not? However, I'm sure the cook you have where you live can teach you a few things."

She leaned back in her chair. "I know what you're thinking. Rich girls can't cook, or do many things."

"I never said a word."

"No, you didn't. You act like a gentleman all of the time, but we both need to relax. I promise you right now you're off duty, and it's only the two of us. " Shawn gave her a doubtful smile, as Kristina pointed toward the couch. "Let's drink the rest of the wine there, and perhaps I can convince you that what goes on here, stays here."

The invitation was tempting, but could he trust himself? "I have no TV, and the only music I have is easy relaxing music I listen to before I go to sleep."

"The music sounds good. What I would like to know, however, is more about you."

Shawn walked over to the couch and moved to one end. She didn't hesitate to sit close to him, invading his space. "There's not much to say."

"There's always a story. It seems like I need to challenge you to a game of dare."

Shawn couldn't control the sudden desire to laugh. "I don't think so. Just ask me, and I'll answer what I can."

"Okay, why no girlfriend?"

Shawn chuckled at the brassy nature. "Do I get to ask such questions?"

"Absolutely."

With his challenge answered, he considered the question before answering, "I've never had time to have a serious relationship. I've worked hard all of my life."

"Everyone works hard, but it doesn't stop the world from spinning around."

"My dad disappeared before I was born, leaving my mom and me to fend for our self."

"I'm sorry. Does your mother not have any other family?"

"She had a father who shunned her. The hard work eventually led to her early death, and there was nothing I could do about it."

"Let me asks you this, if I may. What are your

plans for the future?"

"I've been saving my money, and I hope to start my own business one day." Wow. He wished he had not said that. Such information wouldn't be well received if his grandfather heard it. He needed this job until then. "I hope you tell no one about this."

"I can keep a secret, and I think you know many of my dark secrets already."

"It's my job to protect you, which means I have to know certain things."

"So, are you being nice to me simply because *it's your job*?"

"It's easy to be nice to you, and I know what you're going through. I wish I could do more to protect you." While sounding only like words, he did mean it.

"You know, I have been thinking about this for a while. Many people act like they care about me, but sometimes I think they're only concerned about what problems I might cause them. There's a major difference." She snuggled closer and sipped her wine.

"I know you have been involved with Jeff for a while, and I'm sorry it didn't work out for you."

She laughed in a playful, but almost scornful way. "That relationship was a total farce. My dad would love to see it happen, but he's not for me. Since I had no boyfriend, and had to attend many functions, it was a matter of convenience. Okay, we had a few moments, but that was it."

"I'm sorry to hear that."

"I think it should be obvious. He never calls to check on me. With all of this going on, I would think he would, but no."

Shawn raised his glass and extended it to her. "I guess all people have the same problems, but in different forms."

Kristina raised her glass and finished it before shifting closer. "Can you hold me for a while? With you I feel more secure than I have in a long time. I want to close my eyes and enjoy the music." Since he said nothing, she slid closer until he reached his arm around her. Cuddling would be nice, but not for long.

Kristina pulled a blanket higher to keep warm as a pillow stuffed under her head begged her to dig in deeper. The support under her left much to be desired as she stretched. That's when she realized she was sleeping on the couch. She forced her eyes to open, only to see Lucy standing guard over her. A leash lay beside her. "I see you're ready for your run."

As she turned to watch Shawn stretching into one pose after another, she had a sudden urge to get him to teach her how he did this. The control he had in his movements entranced her as she studied his well toned body. Big muscular guys never did anything for her, but nice abs did. She found herself fantasizing about making love with him, as his body moved in one precise rhythm after another. While he had no fat anywhere, he wasn't skinny either. For her, he had the perfect body she would love to explore.

After he finished he walked over to Lucy who raised her head. "Good morning, girl." Shawn motioned to the open window above them. "Yes, it's beautiful outside."

Kristina rubbed Lucy's head, which she discovered she loved. "How far do you run?"

"Perhaps around five miles, why?"

"I thought about running with you." He gave her a questionable look. "I'm not in too bad shape, I run in the gym . . . some." She raised her arms to her side and pumped them as if she was running

"This may, or may not be such a good idea."

"I have a jogging suit and can wear a hood; no one will know it's me."

"We'll see." He knew the chances of being caught by the media this early in the morning while doing something she had not done before were slim. "You have to keep up with us."

"Is that a challenge?"

"More. It's a requirement." He slipped on a hooded top also. "I have a plan which will help some. I can make some circles while you rest, if you need to."

"Give me five minutes."

Kristina pushed her hair inside the hood and pulled the cord. It felt hard to believe she would allow herself to be in public like this, but no one would see her. She followed Shawn out a small door and alley to a main street.

He reached for her hand. "Let's walk until we merge in with everyone." A block later he pulled her beside him as he increased to a small jog.

The air fresh from the night swept across her face as the traffic slowly moved along. Most New Yorkers never get up this early; she never did. The pace covered several blocks quickly until she soon saw the corner of Central Park, where she glanced at one of Trump's building before bouncing down a set of stairs to the park.

The park always looked like a different world inside the city, as a flock of ducks flew across it. Being a quieter side of the city, she could even hear the sound of their feet pounding the pathway. Her legs started wearing fast, but her lungs felt fine. As she glanced at Shawn, who maintained an even gait while looking ahead, she pressed on, determined to show him she could stay even with him.

After coming to a large circle around a small pond, he motioned for her to take the leash. "Here, stay with Lucy, and I'll make several loops while you catch your breath."

"Don't worry about me; I can keep up with you."

"I know, but Lucy needs a break."

Kristina looked at Lucy, who remained still beside her. "I think she'll be fine, but we'll take it easy for her." She turned to run the loop, but at a smaller pace. Yes, Shawn had found a way for her to save face and still enjoy the morning.

On the second loop three black men emerged out of a side trail and rushed toward her. "Hello, Baby, what have you got there?" Her heart fluttered as she searched for Shawn, who was now coming on a dead run.

As the tall one with a beard came closer, Lucy growled and he backed away. With a smile he opened a knife. "Don't make me kill your fucking dog."

Shawn ran next to her and stopped, as the three men scattered to both sides. She noticed knifes in their hands also. "Okay, we can do this the easy way, or the hard way. We haven't had any white candy in a while." The tall black man stared at her from her feet to her head, obviously intent on intimidating her.

When the guy in the center stepped forward, Shawn met him and kicked head high, planting his foot into his nose and sending blood flying. Lucy also rushed for him as Kristina held the leash.

The short fat guy on the left moved next as Shawn quickly grabbed his hand and twisted it, causing the knife to hit the ground. The man struggled until Shawn twisted again, sending him to the ground on both knees where he yelled, "Fuck you."

Shawn dropped him and turned to the last black guy who swirled his knife, "There will be another day, white boy!"

"I don't think so. Shawn retrieved a gun from behind his back and his badge. "You're all going to jail. Down on the ground, now! I have every reason to use lethal force." He leveled the gun between his eyes.

The whites of his eyes widen as he dropped the knife. "I'm unarmed now."

Shawn cocked the hammer. "Don't push me. Hit the ground now."

The man changed his mind and dropped to the ground as the other two continued to moan.

Shawn reached in his pocket and pulled out his phone. "I have a mugging in Central Park. I provide private security and we're safe, but we wish to push charges." He glanced at Kristina. "I'm sorry, but we have to do this."

This would mean publicity, something she didn't need. She shook until the police arrived.

A stocky policeman rushed over to Shawn. "I thought you would be the one involved in this. What do you want to do with these guys? They will be back on the street by this afternoon."

"I'll leave it in your hands. I would love to not have the news hear about it."

"I'll take care of it, but you owe me for this." Several other policemen rushed in to join them. "Now get out of here and quit causing me more work."

Shawn reached for Kristina's hand and pulled her along with him. "What was that all about?"

"Let's say this isn't the first time I've had problems in the park, but it has been a while. The police hate paperwork as much as everyone. He'll make sure they don't come back, off the record."

They moved quickly until they entered the street above the park. "I have one treat for you now." He held her hand and walked several block allowing her to cool down before stopping in a small bagel shop. He entered and ordered bagels and a treat for Lucy, which she gobbled in seconds.

"That was scary."

"Sorry, my fault, I should have not taken you with me."

"You do know how to handle yourself. Very impressive."

"Maybe, but a true bodyguard would never allow a client to get in such danger, so I did wrong, and I'm sorry."

He called her a client. Is that what he really felt she was? Yes, in a way she was, but she hoped *friend* would be a better choice of words. Still, he squeezed her hand. That you didn't do with clients.

Chapter 15

Shawn stopped at the front desk of an Italian restaurant he had seen before from the outside, but never from the inside. "I'm here to pick up a takeout for Ms. Sutherland."

"Yes, it will be ready in one minute. We don't normally do carry outs, but she's a very good customer of ours." The hostess dressed in a short black dress turned to walk away. She had a great body which he studied. It had been a long time since he had been satisfied, and he had been aroused all day. Having a beautiful woman in his place didn't help, since he daydreamed about what could happen all day.

He had called Kristina several times during the day. She seemed perfectly fine, staying in his place reading a book. It was too bad he had to do work during the day, since he would have loved to spend it with her. His mind had created one scene after another of her being with him.

The hostess returned and handed him the package. "I think you'll enjoy it, and I almost forgot . . . she wanted this wine to go with it." She handed him a bottle.

"Thanks, I'm sure it'll be great." Her low cut dress revealed fantastic cleavage of firm breasts perfectly proportioned for her body. The dress design teased him with the hope of seeing one nipple, but it never did.

Shawn watched the hostess eye him up and down

as he turned. It felt nice to be noticed. Maybe he did have something a girl might like. As he walked he noticed he had a hard on, surely she didn't notice. He hadn't been able to control it all day. He needed relief since his hormones were running crazy.

He soon walked into his place and instead of Lucy running to meet him she stayed next to Kristina who was rubbing her head. "You wouldn't be stealing my best friend, would you?"

"I might, I think she likes me. How was your day?" She had dressed in another outfit he hadn't seen before, a long white dress that looked out of place in his apartment. This is where sweat clothes and old outfits felt good. Still, she looked good as it showed off her body well. It fit tight around her middle and flared at the bottom. A large tie behind her head lifted the front, and the cross pulling design of the material helped to separate each breast and lift them. This reinforced his assumptions of their size and shape.

"It was a normal day. Everyone decided to leave me along for once." He glanced around his place which now looked different. She had spent the day cleaning and placing everything in neat piles. It was never that much of a mess, but it could use a woman's touch.

"I hope you don't mind me cleaning a little." She looked proud of her work.

"It looks incredible. You shouldn't have. You're the only person to ever see this place, and I assume you will be the last. In fact, I intended to not let anyone ever see it, since it has been kind of my private hideaway."

"I think that's why I like it. Who would have

thought such a place would exist right here in the city, and so close to Central Park too. I see you picked up dinner."

"Yes, and they insisted I take this bottle of wine."

"It looks like we're all set. Are you hungry?"

"Yes, I am." He lifted the bag and started to set the table as she stepped over to him. "Why don't you make yourself comfortable and I'll get it ready." She pointed to his office suit.

"I do need to change, and I hope you don't mind if I wear my old duds. I don't have the wardrobe you have."

"To tell the truth, I wish I had some old clothes to lounge around in."

"Are you sure?"

"Yes, I'm sure. If you had a girlfriend over here, what would she be wearing?" He started to say something, but smiled instead. "I saw that smile. What were you thinking?"

"No, you wouldn't like it."

"Try me."

"I . . . was wondering how you would look in one of my old shirts with your hair combed out and not up so professionally."

"Why, you don't like my clothes, or is it my hair?"

"No, both are fine. They're too nice to lounge around with and have fun."

"I can accept the challenge, if you can stand the difference."

"What challenge?"

He watched her march to his clothes and scan through them. It looked like she was going to be criticizing his clothes next. Instead, she pulled a large jersey from a hanger. "This will do."

"I really didn't mean anything."

"No, you were being honest, which is what I needed. It's up to you to get the dinner ready now." She walked off toward his bathroom. "Give me a few minutes."

Since he only had a few plates, trying to present a decent setting would be hard. He opened a box and searched for something else. The only item he located that he could use was some candles. He tried to make a fancy napkin out of a paper towel but gave up; what he had was all he had.

As he heard the door squeak behind him, he turned to see what she was up to. With his jersey extending down to her knees, it made an interesting impromptu dress. He imagined her fantastic body beneath his old jersey, which had seen better days. It was her hair, however, that was all combed out and hanging natural which made her look different.

"Well say something. Do I look that bad?"

"No, not at all, you look totally different and normal." As they walked toward each other, he continued his examination. "This would definitely be a better way to get you out in public with no one knowing who you are?"

"I don't think that will ever happen. Letting you see me like this is one thing, letting the world see me like this will never happen."

"That's a shame. You look beautiful just like you are."

"Do you think so?"

"Yes." He held out his arm to lead her to the table. "The food looks great."

"And smells out of this world. We'll have to go there one day."

Shawn lowered his head. "After this is over, do you think we could ever see each other out in public?"

"We can do whatever we want. I don't think I'll be the first girl to fall for her bodyguard."

Shawn heard the words, but he knew otherwise. Her father would never allow it, and he had no money to keep her in the luxury she was used to. "It sounds like a good movie or book, but this is real life." He lifted a glass of wine he had poured and handed it to her. "But this is tonight, and it is what we have."

"Sounds like a toast I can drink to." She leaned over, touched his glass and sipped slowly. He could see wheels turning inside her beautiful head.

Kristina loved the compliments, especially from someone who gave them very infrequently. She had fantasized about Shawn all day. Now, with him across from her eating, she needed to put her plan in motion. The rape she had lived through left no emotional scars, other than the thoughts of being violated and not being in control of her body. While she knew others girls would let this ruin their life and the joy of sex, she had made her mind up earlier to not allow that.

She watched him chew the piece of prime rib, as some of the juice covered his lip before he used a napkin. He had manners in a distinct way, and not much different from other men she knew, but displayed with more sincerity.

She raised her glass and extended it toward him. "I see you found some more candles?"

"Yes." He glanced around his place. "It's amazing

what candle light can do, even in a place like this."

"I think this might be one of the most romantic settings I can remember. I can see this place being converted to a restaurant."

She heard him laugh with the same slow masculine voice she had loved to listen to. "It would take millions to redo this building and entrance. No, I'm glad to have it just like it is."

"I hope we can do this many more times." She glanced at the music box he had. "Do you have anything nice to dance to?"

"I don't have a lot of music, and what I have is easy listen music to relax to while I kind of chill out here."

"That will be perfect."

"I think you also assume I know how to dance." Shawn winked.

"Don't be modest; I think everyone can do a basic two step. I really simply want to be held. Is that wrong?"

Shawn seemed to understand as he stood and walked to her chair. "No, nothing wrong with that."

After she stood, he walked over to the stereo and pulled out a few CD's until he found one he liked. "Dancing to this might be fascinating."

He wasn't kidding as a mother earth type played, displaying many natural outdoor sounds which felt so relaxing and soothing. She melted into his arms, and watched the world fade away while they danced in almost darkness, less the small flicker of candle lights around his place. As she laid her head against his shoulder and pulled him closer with her arm stretched around him, her breasts pushed in closer to him had to be sending him a message. Still, since he acted like a perfect gentleman, she needed to push harder.

She stretched to be able to stand eye to eye with him. His eyes looked deep and penetrating. Why couldn't she see through them to see what kept him so distant? What had someone done to him before? She was the one with issues she wanted to work past. Since knowing she could still enjoy sex and control her life meant a lot to her, and this slow movement by him confused her, it made her more determined than ever to seduce him.

She studied his lips, opened her mouth, and gave every indication of wanting to be kissed, but still he lingered. While she had to know what he was thinking, and she had no doubt they would make love at some time tonight, she wanted to know he wanted her like she wanted him.

She leaned over and whispered in his ear. "You're a very unique individual, and I don't think I've ever met anyone like you. You don't let many people get close to you, do you?"

"I've learned to be somewhat of a loner."

"Hey, I don't bite, and if you're worried about my father hearing about this, it will not be from me." She pulled away from his ear to study his face and analyze his grin—the beginning crack to a wall she wanted to tear down.

Without hesitation she moved closer to him and felt his hot breath against her face. With his lips barely inches from hers, she waited, anticipating what he would do. As he yielded, he brushed his lips against her lips in a small, but oh so significant advance. Moments later they melted more firmly this time. He had strong, powerful lips she enjoyed caressing with hers.

As she floated to the music, she sucked on his lower lip, and breathed in a deeper appreciation of his scent. The effect of the wine caused her to stumble to the steps, but he held her tight enough to keep from worrying about falling.

While she kissed his lips, she also ran her fingers through his hair and studied the feel of its soft straight texture. His dark blond hair looked good, but would even look better if he would allow it to grow longer.

When he finally leaned over to kiss her neck, a move he initiated on his own, he sent waves of heat over her body. She couldn't have wanted anyone more than him as she slowly pulled him to the couch where she sat almost on top of him before wrapping a leg over his. His shirt she wore rode high on her leg. "I hope you don't mind me being so aggressive. It's just that . . . I need to know the guy who raped me hasn't ruined my attitude toward sex. I want to know that I'm in control, and that I can choose my own destiny."

"I understand, I think." He acted skittish. "I need to mention one thing."

"Which?"

"I haven't had a girlfriend in a long time and well . . . I don't have any protection here."

She knew she shouldn't laugh, but it was funny. "Not a problem, I can wait on you to make a trip to the store. Also, you don't have to think I'll break; I'm fully in control of what I want, and the baby will not be affected by sex, if that's what you're worried about."

He leaned over and kissed her much more

passionate than earlier. "I'll be back in a few minutes." She had his motor running hot. Tonight would be unbelievable.

Chapter 16

As soon as Shawn walked in to his office he saw the note to come to the boardroom. What now? He knew if it was a big emergency, they would have called him on his cell phone. As he prepared to leave, the previous night flashed through his head. He loved it, but knew he shouldn't have. Too much was at risk.

After he rushed upstairs to the boardroom, he was stopped by Kelly outside the entrance. "I'm glad I caught you before you went in."

"What's up?"

"They know you and Kristina are spending a lot of time together, and they want some answers. Brent is particularly upset, since he heard about you having problems in Central Park."

"Oh, I see, I can explain that." He glanced around her at the door. "Who else is in there?"

"Lawson and a couple of the fathers of some of the boys on the cruise. They all want to know when the DNA test will be completed. They're also having a heated debate on if she will have an abortion. I hate to say it, but it would be the best thing for everyone. She really doesn't plan on having an illegitimate baby, does she?"

"That will be her decision." He tried to sound neutral.

"I know being raped can be a horrifying thing for anyone to go through, but since she doesn't remember anything, it would have been much better if she hadn't discovered she was pregnant. That's the only reason she knows she was raped, isn't it?"

Shawn did some thinking about what has confused him for a while. He thought a guy who raped her wouldn't take the time to clean her up and redress her, unless he knew the drug would totally erase her memory. It wasn't the kind of thing you could call maid services for.

"At this time we don't know all of the answers as to who her attacker was, or were. It's strange she woke the next morning fully dressed."

"Maybe this isn't where she became pregnant. Have you considered this?"

"She insists she hasn't had sex with anyone else, and that this is the only night she couldn't remember anything."

"Being the legal counsel for the company, I would appreciate you sharing with me anymore news you receive. I've tried to stay out of this until now. I had hoped she would simply have an abortion, and this would all disappear."

"She has pressures come from many directions, but above all what she needs is our support."

"Okay, but for now you're on the firing line. Let's go on in."

Shawn walked in and heard the discussions come to a grinding halt. "I think you wanted to see me."

Brent stood. "Yes, we need to ask you some questions. I had the police contact me last night. It appears you had a run in with a few guys in the park a day ago. Would you like to tell us about that?"

"Not much to tell. I was attacked while running in the park. I held them there until the police arrived.

They said they would take care of it for me. Why? Is there a problem?"

Brent looked at Lawson. "I think we also heard you had a woman with you. Was that Kristina?"

Shawn didn't know how they knew this, but he couldn't lie. "I think you must already know it was." He turned toward Lawson. "I'll assure you sir; she was never in any danger."

Lawson waved at Brent to retake his seat. "I'm trusting you with my daughter's life."

"Yes, sir, and I know you are."

"I'm very apprehensive as to not knowing where she's being kept."

"I'll assure you she's somewhere safe."

Lawson looked around the room. "From what I've heard, the results will be back in a few days, and we'll finally know the truth. Brent wants you removed from this until this is over, but I want you to stay on it. My daughter trusts you, and that's important to me."

The other men on the board leaned forward, but said nothing.

"I'm still investigating all avenues I can on this, and hope to get a break soon. Kristina still hasn't decided if she's going to have an abortion or not. If she decides to keep the baby, she might need protection for a long time. It's something to be considered."

Brent blurted out with his usual flare. "And another reason she should consider having an abortion. Since she trusts you, perhaps you could help her see that."

"I've heard many arguments for the abortion, but how many have we heard for the unborn baby." He turned to face his granddad.

As Shawn opened his mouth, Brent raised a hand. "Okay, I know when I have said too much. I have the well being of the company on my mind, and what I think will be best for Kristina."

One of the other directors stood. "We have also hired additional private detectives who will be conducting investigations. Shawn, we expect you to give them your full cooperation."

"I understand, and any help will be appreciated. I hope they know to keep this information secure."

"I'm sure they will, and this has nothing to do with your ability. We know how busy you've been providing coverage for Kristina."

Brent shut a file he carried with him "I think that will do it for today. Shawn, I would like a word with you after the meeting."

"Yes, sir, I'll be in your office in a few minutes."

Shawn walked out and down the stairs to his office. He needed to clear his head before he confronted his grandfather. What did he have on his mind? He checked his phone and saw several messages. He paused to see who they were from. Not surprising, one of them was from Kristina, wanting to know what was going on. He would have to call her later. A small photo of his mother seemed to be speaking to him. She had more morals than anyone he knew. He wished he could ask her for advice. He shut his eyes for a minute before heading back up stairs to face the music.

Brent's secretary stopped him as he went in. "He's in a bad mood, so watch yourself."

He had already suspected such as he walked in and

stood by the chair in front of his desk. Brent stayed turned sideways, looking out a window. He looked much older than usual with his hair uncombed, something very unusual for him. Finally Brent turned to face him. "Shut the door and have a seat."

Shawn returned to the door and shut it. While he needed to stand, he selected a seat, for now anyway.

"You have worked hard with the company, and I know you mean well. My legacy here is almost over. I also know you probably hate me for what I did in the past, and I can't say I really blame you. However, ruining this company with a scandal isn't good for anyone, and that's what will happen if this isn't contained soon."

Shawn glanced at the ceiling. "And I think you know my response."

"You can have a future here after I'm gone."

"You mean I get to finally acknowledge my birthright after you're gone?"

"Something like that. If I bring your past out into the open now, the scandal will destroy this company."

"Is that . . . destroy the company . . . or destroy you?"

"Unfortunately, they're one and the same. You need to work with me on this."

"I noticed how you want to *work with me* on this. Why are you trying to have me fired?"

"I wouldn't let that happen and . . . if it did, I can send you money to live on, if that's what you want."

"No, I have paid my own way all of my life; as you know."

"And you're never going to let me forget that, are you?"

"You know, mother forgave you a long time ago. It's going to take a longer time for me to do the same."

While hardened from years of self denial, Shawn studied a tear in the corner of the old man's eye. *Am I finally getting through to him after all of these years? Would he ever fully admit what he did was wrong?*

Brent turned back to the window. "Bundle up, Shawn, I think we're going to have some storms coming soon."

Chapter 17

Kristina waited in the doctor's office, as she struggled with the anticipated results. The DNA tests were back and he had the results. With so many possibilities to consider, she had lost sleep all night working out responses to each. After making love to Shawn, she curled inside his embrace, but only managed to hear him sleeping peacefully. Still, his warmth kept her calm.

The doctor entered with a frown. "We've been over and over these results, and there's not a match. I'm sorry."

"No, this can't be right." Her mind flashed to new possibilities as her head became dizzy.

"Are you okay?"

"Give me a minute. Do we need to redo the test?"

"I think we have a good DNA on the baby, but we don't have a match for a possible dad. The good news is that the baby appears to be perfectly fine with no genetic problems."

Kristina smiled at the news, knowing her baby might have a chance of a normal life. "Do we have samples from all of the men on the yacht?"

"That . . . you'll have to ask someone else. I did hear some of the older men, considered much too old for you, were excluded. You know several of the board members are in their seventies."

Kristina squirmed in her seat. "Surely that wouldn't happen." She slumped in her seat, trying to focus.

"As I said, the baby's doing fine. I hope you do decide to give your baby a chance."

"Perhaps, but I still don't know. I mean like, what will it look like? Not knowing who the father is will make this difficult. I need some time to think."

"I can offer you something to help you relax that will not hurt the baby."

"No, I'll be fine. Tell Shawn to get me out of here."

Shawn listened to the results and shook his head. Something didn't add up. He would have to recheck the passenger and staff list. Someone was not accounted for. He drove along the street and made several detours to make sure no one was following him before he turned down the alley to the small loading dock inside his building.

Since he had downloaded every piece of evidence onto his laptop, he would start from the beginning and reanalyze it all. Kristina remained motionless as he came to a stop and turned off the motor. After he closed the garage door, he slipped back into the car, waiting on her to think through her emotions and anger.

She leaned over to him after a long time. "My baby's not going to have a daddy, and may never know who it is. I can't imagine."

Actually he could. He had never seen his father. "This isn't over yet. We need to get you inside."

Lucy waited on them as they walked in, waging her tail as usual. Shawn watched Kristina smile for the first time. Good for Lucy. He helped her walk to the couch, where they had spent hours enjoying each other's company over the last few days.

Shawn knew it was only late afternoon and he should return to the office for a while, but he felt bad about leaving her there. "What can I get you?"

"Nothing for now. When you get back a big bottle of booze would be good."

Shawn looked at her, and raised an eyebrow. "Maybe this is not a good idea with you being pregnant."

"I think I deserve it. I'll have you here to make sure I don't totally overdo it. You'll look out for me, won't you? I know I need to do better."

"I'll be here for you. I can call the office and tell them I won't be back today."

"No, you need to go. I know this will be hard, but I need to call my dad and let him know what I learned."

"Maybe it would be better if you were alone for a while, but if you want me to take you to see him, I can."

"No, definitely not. I need time to think."

"Okay, in such a case, I'll be back in a few hours."

As he leaned next to her she reached over to kiss him before reminding him, "Don't forget the booze."

Her kiss was becoming more and more natural. Breaking it off with her one day would be hard, and getting harder to imagine every day.

Shawn checked his office for messages. No one had called. He checked the schedule, and there were no board meetings planned or outings he had to know about. The extra guards made his life easy, but he knew that wouldn't last forever, and he would be back into working long hours again soon.

He opened a drawer and studied the phone Kristina had allowed him to keep for her, which had the original message on it demanding that she have an abortion. He played it several times, but could not place the voice, which had been altered. He studied the phone and its many applications she had downloaded.

He clicked on the camera function and stopped. He had never looked at what photos she had taken. He glanced around and closed the door. She might not like him prying, but it might be fun to see what she had on it. He examined many photos of her with girlfriends at a bar drinking. He settled into his chair and continued flipping until his phone rang.

"Shawn, this is Kelly. I have some news I wanted to pass on to you. The investigators hired by some of the board members have come across some information you might want to see."

"What is it?"

"Photos of Kristina out partying. They have interviewed some of the guys in the photos, and were told she was known to have gone home with several of them. The story Kristina told about not having sex with anyone may be a lie."

"I have a hard time believing that."

"I know you're getting close to Kristina, but how well do you really know her?"

"Of course I've not known her for long, but over the last few days I've learned a lot about her. Are any of these guys willing to take a DNA test?"

"Shawn you can't make all of the guys in New York have a DNA test, you know that."

He held his breath. He knew Kristina didn't have

sex with one guy after another. This made it sound like she was a tramp, and he knew better. "I would still like to see the information they have. Can you e-mail it to me?"

"Sure. When will you see Kristina again?"

"She wanted to call her dad and give him the news on the DNA. It was hard on her to learn we didn't have a match."

"I know. Her father called me after they talked."

Shawn scratched his head as he wondered who else knew. Word travels fast. "I know we haven't checked everyone on board the yacht."

"Yes, but with this new information I don't think you'll get anyone else to submit a sample for testing."

"I guess I'm back to where we started. Let me talk to Kristina, and I'll see what the board wants me to do tomorrow."

"Call me if you need me, Shawn."

###

Kristina hated her father's voice and his way of lecturing her. Whatever happened, she would not go back to living there. It was time that she moved out and was on her own and maybe even leave New York. The world was a large place.

Her father called her an embarrassment for accusing someone on the yacht, and he had sided with the views of the other investigators. Yes, she liked to party and play with some of the guys who ran around town, but she never screwed any of them.

Where was Shawn? Baby or no baby, she wanted to get plastered tonight. If she decided to leave town, she hoped he would help her. He had always been so supportive, and she needed him.

Lucy was resting below her on the floor. Since she had never had a dog before, she would see about finding her own when she moved out. She even imagined her father giving her his blessing in moving, especially her mother, who had been quiet the whole time. They would have a lot to deal with when the scandal erupts.

Lucy picked up her ears. "Hey, girl, do you hear Shawn coming?" The sound of someone running the stairways confirmed her suspicions. She breathed deeply with a new sense of peace. He was coming home. A funny word for where she was hiding out, but still home in an intimate way that she needed.

Shawn pushed through the door. "I'm sorry it took me so long to get home, but I had several calls at the office." He walked over and hugged her immediately. "I'm so sorry for everything today."

"It's not your fault I got this major problem."

"How did your father take the news?"

"Not good. He and everyone in New York think I'm a slut out partying and sleeping with every stud in town."

"We both know better. I've done some thinking, and we need to find out who's behind these attacks, and . . . why he wants you to have an abortion so bad."

"That could be a lot of people. I have many jerks wanting me to abort. Maybe that's why I'm fighting it so much. I don't like being told what to do."

Shawn reached for a piece of paper. "I'm going to make a full list. Please excuse me, but I'll spare no one. First, your parents would rather see the problem disappear, several members of the board of directors, especially those with young sons, my . . . main boss at the company, Brent, and to a lesser extent Jeff. And this puzzles me. Since he was dating you for a while, I would think he would take a more active role in this investigation."

"Many people read more into the relationship than was really there. I think he wants to distance himself to make sure no one blames him for this."

"I hate to ask this, but is there anyone else we can add to this list?"

"Only the unthinkable. Several members of the board didn't submit samples. You don't think one of the older board members would have done this, do you?"

"Very slim."

"Shawn, I was thinking before you walked in. If I decide to move to another town, would you help me get settled in?"

"That's a little extreme, don't you think?"

"No, not really. I don't really have anyone else to help me."

"You know, I'll do what I can."

"I know, and that's why I feel like I can trust you more than anyone else." She leaned over and hugged him tight. "Please, never leave me."

###

Never was an interesting word. It sounded like commitment, but one he might make. "I'm here for you."

Kristina looked at the bag he had with him. "What do you have?"

"Some work for tonight, but I'll get to it later. And some *booze* for you, as you asked. You know . . . I'll not let you have too much. Someone needs to look out for the baby." He reached over and felt of her stomach which was still flat and sexy, but radiating a special energy he could connect with. Being a father would be fantastic one day.

True to his word, he watched her carefully, but as he suspected a few drinks quickly allowed her to sleep. He carried her to the bed where he undressed her before covering her. He wondered if when she drank, she often passed out. Is that what really happened? No one had to use a date drug. Maybe someone offered her too many drinks, knowing this.

He moved to the table, where he kept his computer and turned it on. After checking his e-mail, he saw the photos sent to him by the other investigators. They showed Kristina out on the town, much like the photos he had seen on her cell phone camera.

As he analyzed each photo, he recognized no one, until he studied one photo of her being offered a drink. He enlarged the photo to see Josh, one of the sons of a board member. So, they knew each other before that night. How much contact did they have on the yacht? Still, he had submitted a DNA sample and there was no match. That is, unless it wasn't his, or it had been contaminated in some way.

He lifted her phone out of his bag and connected it to his computer so that he could see better on the larger screen. He flipped one photo after another until the scene changed. He recognized the photos in minutes. She had taken some aboard the yacht. New life surged though his body as he glanced over at her sleeping peacefully behind him. Good, he might be up all night.

Kristina woke slowly as she reached beside her, but she couldn't find Shawn's warm body she loved to snuggle next to in the morning. *Where is he?* As she stretched, the smell of coffee drifting across the room helped to revitalize her. *How much did I have to drink the night before?*

She blinked her eyes several time as she focused on the light hanging over the computer table and Shawn. "Don't tell me you stayed awake all night."

She watched him stand and smile with his white teeth gleaming from the one spot light focused on him. "Something like that. It's still early. You need to get some more sleep."

"I miss my cuddle partner." She moved to one side to make room for him. "Please come to bed."

He reached above him and flipped off the light. "Since I assume that's an order."

"You're damn right it is. I need you."

In the dim light she watched him strip down to nothing and slip under the cover. With his body still cold from the night, she needed to warm him instead, but she didn't mind. They would melt together soon enough. His skin sent her body into spasms of joy. She never could get enough of him, and tonight, well early morning, would be no different.

As he snuggled closer she wrapped a leg over his. Raising it higher until she placed it over his stomach, the feel of his dick aroused her. She massaged his chest as her mind raced ahead. She loved to make love to him, since he obligated her with every need she had. His patience and gentleness marked everything she needed in a man.

When his hand touched her leg, she moaned. She

wanted him to have no doubt what she wanted. If he would touch her, he would soon discover she was already wet. He had to do nothing to excite her, since she was already there and more.

As he rolled over closer to her, she knew this was more than a fling, or a short affair that would quickly disappear. She opened herself to him and trusted that he would see it also. Suspecting he had reservations, she would break through and gain his trust soon. Then, the world would be perfect.

After making love for a long time, they fell asleep until the morning light woke them and Lucy whimpered for them to get up. She knew Lucy had to go early in the mornings. "Okay, lover boy, we need to get moving."

She watched Shawn rub his eyes. "What time is it?"

She glanced at the clock on the table. "It's almost eight."

"Wow, I stayed up too late last night. I need to move fast, but first I want to go over something with you." He jumped from the bed and rushed to his computer. "While I take Lucy outside, I want you to look at these photos you took on the yacht."

"Why, what did you find?"

"Maybe nothing, but maybe everything." He picked up the leash. "I'll be back in a few minutes."

Kristina moved toward the computer and flipped through the photos. She had forgotten about taking these photos. After watching everyone enjoying champagne, a sickening feeling overtook her as she remembered some of the details.

What was it Shawn noticed that she needed to? She

soon picked out the three young sons of the board members as they acted silly, and they were always toasting their glasses together. She had taken several shots of them.

Shawn soon returned. "Do you recognize anyone?"

"Yes, I think I know everyone, why?"

"These young guys are all drinking heavily, don't you think?"

"Look closer, their glasses are always full, and they have more than one glass, especially this one guy here." He tapped on one guy's picture with a pen.

"Yes, that's Josh. He's a little strange, and I heard he was gay at one time. The last time I saw him was the night we went to the Manhattan Club, where he had a new girlfriend."

"Interesting. What did he have to say to you there?"

"We didn't talk. I simply remember him staring at me. I thought it was the fact he was under suspicion because he was asked to take one of the DNA tests."

"When we headed out of the Club did you see him there?"

"No, but I don't remember looking for him either."

Shawn returned to flipping photos. "Take a look at this photo."

"Do you mean the one where he's taking another glass from the cocktail waitress?"

"Yes, and look at his other hand; the one holding a full glass. I would venture he's taking the glass for someone else."

"Many people were handing me drinks, I think he may have given me one."

"Or perhaps several, while he only pretended to

drink."

"So, you think he was trying to get me drunk."

"That's what it looks like. I have more photos taken by others on the yacht. I hope to be able to piece them together, but it will take more time. I need to get to my office. Do me a favor and don't say anything until I have this pulled together."

"Sure, but you know his DNA came back with a negative match."

"He might not be the rapist, but I now suspect he knows more than he's telling. I'd love to get him back in my office for a few questions."

"Good luck on getting past his dad."

"This is one reason I want to keep my suspicions to us for now."

"Okay, I'll trust your judgment." Kristina pulled Shawn's jersey, which she had permanently stolen from him, closer around her neck. "I want to go with you. It'll be harder for him to lie if he knows I'm there. If he holds some answers, I deserve to know what happened."

"This might not be a good idea to have you confront him, but it might work. Let me talk to him first, and I'll decide what's best then."

"Good, I can pretend to be calling on my dad. I haven't seen him for several days." As Kristina thought about what she would say to her dad, she knew he would ask where she had been staying. That would be too much of a shock to disclose to him now.

Chapter 18

Shawn said goodbye to Kristina as he left her on the elevator. He had decided the best person to call for help was Kelly. She might want to know what he was up to, but he knew she had some pull. Since calling Josh's dad would get him nowhere, he dialed Kelly's number.

"Kelly, this is Shawn. I have something I'm working on and need some help. I need to talk to Josh and see if he can help me."

"I thought this case of rape on the yacht was closed. What are you working on?"

"Tell Josh the DNA has cleared him, but he might know something that will help me."

"Such as?"

"I think he might know who the rapist is. I'm still convinced it's someone on the boat."

"All of the men were tested for a match."

"Not all of the men. This was a voluntary submission. If you don't call him, I'll have to."

"I understand, let me see what I can do."

"Kristina's with me, but on her way to see her father now. Also, Josh doesn't need to know what I'm suspicious of so just tell him I need his help."

Shawn quickly shifted through other photos he had collected. It appeared Josh was in the middle of the drinking. He had an extra glass he was attempting to give to someone. Shawn assumed somehow he had managed to get the drug into it. It might be that the other guys were in with him on this.

Josh's father soon called Shawn. "Hi, I heard you wanted to see my son."

"Yes, I'm trying to identify some people in some photos, and I hoped he might be able to help me."

"I think many people can help you with identifying people, but he's in the building now. I think he was on his way to see Brent."

"Okay, perhaps I'll run into him in a minute. Kristina's in with her dad now, and I need to report in with Lawson also. If you see Lawson, let him I know I need to ask him some questions about what he remembers about people drinking that night."

"I will. I know he wants to clear this up more than anyone."

After climbing the stairs and entering the executive floor Shawn heard a loud pop sound, but his instincts told him it could have been a gun shot. He pulled his pistol and ran along the hallway, where several people were venturing out to see what had happened. When a loud scream came from down the hall he ran quicker, until he saw several people blocking the doorway to Brent's office.

He pushed inside and to where he saw Brent, who was slumped over his desk with blood pooling around him. He heard another scream when a second secretary rounded the corner. Shawn turned to the crowd. "Someone call for an ambulance and the police." He ushered one guy out who he quickly recognized as Josh. "No one touch anything."

He rushed to his grandfather, suspecting his grandfather was dead before he reached him. With a gun rested in his grandfather's hand, Shawn felt sick.

Why would he do that?

He made sure not to touch anything important, but stored mental notes on everything in his office. The gun was in his left hand, but he knew he was right handed. He put his gun away as the shock set in. His grandfather was gone.

The police soon arrived and shut everything down on the executive floor. Shawn had already ordered the front door to the building locked by the guard stationed there. He made notes as fast as he could on who was near the door to his grandfathers office.

Shawn heard Kristina's screams as she rushed in with her father. He ran to her to keep her from seeing and held her tight as he walked her to another room. He knew everyone would have to know they now had a special relationship. He would explain later, but she didn't need to have nightmares from this. He would deal with his own later. Words he wanted to say to his grandfather, he would never have the chance now.

Chapter 19

As Kristina stumbled to another office, her body trembled from the sight of the blood. She had been around Brent for all of her life, and he felt almost like an uncle. Why would he shoot himself like that, and why now? She squeezed Shawn's hand as he made phone calls.

A secretary leaned over to her. "Here let me help you for a minute. I know Shawn's going to be busy." She looked at Shawn, and knew he would be.

"Shawn, why?"

"I don't know. Please stay here; you'll be okay. I need to do some things."

"I understand." She watched Shawn walk out, knowing he would return later. She turned to the secretary. "Can you find my father?"

"I'm sure he'll be here soon. Is there anything I can get you?"

"No. I'll be fine.

Shawn finally walked back in. "Come on, I want you to wait in my office until we get this under control." He held her hand as they quickly walked the stairs. "I want you to see some photos." He opened the computer and pointed to the screen. "I'll be back soon."

As he stood to leave, Kelly walked in. "We need to talk."

"Yes, but I need to go to the police station for a while and give a statement."

"I can't believe he killed himself." She leaned over and cried.

"I'm not so sure he did."

"What do you mean?" She looked shocked.

The gun was in his left hand, he's right handed."

"I didn't notice that." She backed away from the desk.

"Kelly, I saw you when I walked in. Who else was in his office when you got there, or were you the first?"

"I was second. Josh was ahead of me. He had made an appointment to see Brent. I'm not sure why, but I heard they had heated words earlier." Kelly looked directly at Shawn. "I think he was shot before Josh walked in. Brent's secretary could verify that."

"I plan to talk to her soon."

"As the company attorney, did Brent have any contact with any attorney's lately, or did he have a will?"

"He had his own personal attorney, and I'm sure he did. He didn't have any next of kin I knew about. I'm sure the police will be checking on this."

"I'm sure they will." Shawn hung his head. "I also know what this will do to the company."

"Yes, it will hurt, since he owned the majority of the stock." Kelly looked at Kristina in front of the computer. "What is she doing on the computer?"

"I have her looking at photos from the cruise."

"Why right now?"

"I think I know who raped Kristina and maybe who's behind Brent's death."

"I'd be careful making assumptions."

"I am, and this is just between us, but the evidence

is staring at us right here." He glanced at the screen.

They all leaned over toward the screen. With several glasses of champagne in his hand, it appeared he was handing out drinks to someone, and that could very well be Kristina, who spoke first. "I do think I had him bring me a drink, but I can't be absolutely sure."

"In any case, I'm sure the police will want to talk to him about Brent's death." He intentionally left off the word suicide. He wasn't sure it was.

Kelly turned toward Shawn. "Josh is the one who supplied the photos of Kristina out on the town." She turned to Kristina, as if to apologize.

"It sounds like he's trying to cover up something."

Kelly stared into space. "What else do you have?"

Shawn had many theories, but wanted to share nothing else at this time. "I have some unanswered questions. I'm sure it will all come out in time."

"I see. I would appreciate it if you would keep me in the loop. This will cause many legal problems for the company." Kelly turned toward Kristina. "For what it's worth, I feel sorry for you and what you had to go through."

As Kelly walked out, a police officer walked in. "I was told you would be here. We need to talk." He looked at Kristina. "Alone for a few minutes."

Kristina smiled. "I understand. I'll see if I can find my dad."

With the door closed, the officer continued, "I understand you're working on a rape case here."

"Possible rape case. We're still gathering information."

"What's the connection to the death upstairs?"

"I'm still working on it, but I don't think it was a suicide."

"I'll agree. I think it would be good for you to come to the station to bring us up to date on what you do know."

"Okay, but I hope you'll share some information with me also."

"Agreed. I know you'll be interviewing one guy who walked in first on the death upstairs. A guy named Josh."

"Yes, we plan to ask him some questions, but since his dad already has an attorney for him we know we won't get many answers."

Shawn continued, "I hear Josh and Brent had a large argument. I would love to know what the dispute was about. I'll be doing my own investigation, and I hope we can share some information. "

The officer appeared to be thinking about it. "I think we can cooperate some here. Is there anything else?"

"There is only one thing that I know will come out at some time, and I hope you can keep this quiet until we have this case solved. I owe it to Kristina to tell her first."

"What is it?"

"No one in the company knows that Brent was my grandfather."

"Wow." He scratched his head. "Are you in your grandfather's will?"

"I know what you're thinking, but my grandfather basically disinherited me and my mother many years ago. It was only a few years ago that he found me and offered me this job. I've no idea if he has a will or not since he never discussed it with me."

"I'm sure all of this will come out. Who saw you when your grandfather was shot?"

"Most of the floor saw me running toward his office. You can verify this with many people."

The officer scribbled some notes. "And what were you doing on the executive floor?"

"I was on the way to find Josh, who was visiting his dad on the executive floor." Shawn pointed to the computer. "I want to show you something. We suspect Kristina may have been given a date rape drug on a cruise. Take a look at the guy holding two glasses of champagne."

"That looks like Josh. We'll need a copy of this."

"No problem. I wanted to ask Josh to come to see me."

"I understand now."

"You said you heard Josh and your granddad had words."

"Yes, Kelly, the company attorney told me this a few minutes ago."

"Did she say what they were about?"

"No, but that's my next step, and one I hope you can find out for me as you interview people. I'll be glad to pass on any information I receive."

The officer closed his pad. "Can you put this all in a full report to me?"

"Sure. I know the board of directors here will also want a copy."

"We'll talk soon."

###

Kristina found her dad visibly shaken in his office. "There you are. I'm so sorry you had to see this."

"I'm fine dad. How are you taking this?"

"Brent was one of my best friends, and I can't believe he would do something like this."

"Shawn doesn't think it was suicide."

"We all saw the gun in his hand seconds after we heard the shot."

"Shawn noticed the gun in his left hand. Have you ever known Brent to use his left hand for anything?"

Lawson slammed his fist on the desk. "No, never. Shawn thinks he was killed? By who?"

"He's working on it." Kristina closed her eyes briefly. "I've had several attempts on my life recently. I'm scared it might be the same person. If it hadn't been for Shawn, I might have also been killed."

"Where is Shawn now?"

"I left him talking to the police. He's doing everything he can to get to the bottom of this."

"I've been worried about you, especially not knowing where you're staying."

"Dad, I've never lied to you before. I'll tell you if you promise not to tell mom."

She watched him hesitate. She kept her silence until he gave in. "Where?"

"I'm staying with Shawn. He has a secure place where he lives."

"I don't think I like this."

"If you say anything to anyone, I'll leave and not tell you where I am. I feel safer with him than anywhere. He's really a great guy also."

Lawson gave her a skeptical eye. "Do you really think this is someone you should have an affair with?"

"Who said anything about an affair?" She glared at her dad. "This is something I think I should decide on my own, don't you?"

"For now, I just want you safe. If you want me to hire additional security for you, I can."

"Dad, I think I have the best right now, trust me."

"If you want me to be part of this, I need to talk to him and you."

"Only if you agree to be nice. I really like him, and I don't want you to ruin this for me."

"We'll see. Okay, I'll do my best for now."

"I'm sure he'll be back after the police leave, but I also know he's looking for Josh."

"Josh has already left. His dad had an attorney here in no time ushering him out of the building."

"Josh was the first one in to see Brent dead. The police will want to talk to him, and there's something else. Shawn thinks he might be responsible for giving me the date rape drug."

Kristina watched the rage in her father return. "But . . . he was cleared when the DNA test returned."

"Shawn thinks he might not be the rapist, but he might have knowledge of what happened."

Her dad straightened his back. "In such a case, I also want to talk to him. I want to see Shawn as soon as you can find him."

His wish came soon, as his secretary buzzed him. "I have Shawn outside, sir."

"Send him in."

Kristina watched Shawn enter as she held her breath, hoping her father wouldn't embarrass her now. To take the initiative, she stood and walked toward Shawn to reinforce her show of support and connection to him. She slipped her hand into his and waited for her father to speak.

"I see you two . . . have been spending some time together. I hope you both know what you're doing."

"My interest is to protect your daughter. I might know who's responsible for her attacks, but I need more proof." Shawn glanced over at her as his eyes remained steady and he stood his ground.

"I understand you have questions for Josh."

"Yes, but I understand his dad has rushed him out of the building, but he won't be able to avoid the police who have questions for him."

"Before this is aired in public, I think it would be good to discuss it here. I hope you have good information, since his dad's not one to confront without justifications."

"I'll not be accusing anyone, only asking questions. Ones . . . I think you'll want to know also."

"Don't say a word, and I'll see if I can get him on the phone." He pressed his intercom button. "See if you can get David Swafford on the phone for me." He paused. "I assume the funeral will be in a few days. We'll need major security at it. This should be a private affair."

"I'll be working on it later today."

The phone rang. "Hello, David, I need to set up a meeting with you and Josh. I hope to do this out of the public spotlight. We're going to have enough problems ahead of us." He listened for a while before answering. "That will be fine if you bring an attorney with you, and we look forward to seeing you at nine tomorrow morning. I'll have Shawn here also, as well as Kelly, if I can arrange it."

"Shawn looked over at Kristina. "I need to get her out of here without being seen. I'm sure the press is all over this place. My guards downstairs can keep them out of the building, but not off the street."

"Yes, I agree. We'll all need help leaving today."

Kristina realized she was still holding Shawn's hand. It had become so natural that she hadn't paid attention to it until she prepared to stand. She watched her father's stare indicating that he had. She didn't care, but she knew that he would have much more to say later. She walked closer to her dad. "Don't worry about me, I promise I'll be safe."

He moved closer and whispered. "I do worry about you. I love you, baby."

"I love you too, dad. You know it." She backed away and reached for Shawn's hand. "We need to go."

Chapter 20

Shawn had shared what he learned with the police the night before. They now had him fully wired for the meeting, just in case Josh broke with what he knew was the truth now. The small conference room on the floor below the executive one helped to keep the meeting private, but he knew several police officers were close by if needed.

He reached over and squeezed Kristina's hand. "It'll be all over soon." He watched Lawson who acted nervous, as a knock signaled the arrival of others. Kelly walked in with Josh and his dad. All had somber faces. Another guy, presumably an attorney, followed closely behind them.

David started first by addressing Shawn. "I hope what you have is worthwhile in dragging us in here." He turned to Lawson. "I hate to say it, but I have more photos of your daughter out on the town. I know what you must be going through not knowing who the father is."

As Shawn watched Lawson tightening his fist, he prepared to move between them if necessary. "Any information is valuable to us. We all simply want the truth."

Josh's dad lowered his head. "First I want to say we're all shocked on the death of Brent yesterday. This has been hard on Josh."

Lawson spoke next. "I'm sure it was. We all heard Josh was on his way to see Brent, and I'm sure there will be many questions raised by others as to why."

The guy stood to confirm who he was. "As Josh's attorney, it might not be good for him to answer these questions."

Lawson leaned over the table. "That is if he's trying to hide something." He directly challenged Josh and his dad.

Josh raised his hand to stop the conversation. "I had heard some of the members of the board of directors were excluded from submitting DNA samples, and I was questioning why. Mr. Lyons heard about me asking questions, and had called me into his office."

Shawn entered the discussion. He had to know more. "Was that the only reason he called you to his office?"

Josh glanced at the attorney. "We had a few words about him being bossy and demanding."

Shawn held his breath before he asked the most important question, "Did you see him pull the trigger?"

Josh responded immediately. "No, it was seconds before I arrived. It scared the hell out of me. At first, I wasn't sure what it was, but I knew it came from his office."

"So . . . you were the first one in his office?" Lawson asked.

"Yes, I know I went into shock. I've never seen so much blood before."

Lawson continued, "Did you touch anything or remove anything?"

"No, others entered behind me in a few seconds." He pointed to Kelly. "I remember you coming behind me, and pulling me back from him."

Kelly had tears flowing. "I remember."

Lawson added the hardest question. "Do you have any idea why he would kill himself?"

"No, he really freaked me out." Josh started shaking,

After several minutes Shawn returned his attention to a screen. "Here's another reason I wanted to have you here. These are photos from the night of the cruise."

The attorney inserted a question. "What does this have to do with the Brent's death?"

"Nothing, but maybe everything." Shawn hit the projection on button as the screen broadcasted the images."We have many of you holding more than one glass of champagne."

His dad spoke first. "I think we were all passing champagne around that night to celebrate."

"Yes, but only one person had to be taken downstairs after a few drinks. By the way, thanks for the photos you brought with you. Here is what doesn't make sense. By your own admission Kristina loves to have a good time like many of us, but she is accustomed to drinking, and has thus built up a good tolerance to alcohol. So . . . why did she become drunk after two glasses of champagne, and especially after the one you gave her, Josh?"

"I didn't give her anything."

Shawn raised his voice. "I have more photos, and I think you do also."

Josh starred at Kristina. "You think you're so above everyone else. So smart. I didn't rape you. As you know I'm gay, and so are the other sons of the board of directors. This is why we all came together."

"So, you drugged her. What else did you do to her?"

The attorney raised a hand to grab attention. "Don't answer that. If you had any involvement in drugging her, you'll also be guilty of rape if some else did."

"I didn't rape her." He jumped from the chair and inched for the door. "I'm not listening to any more of this. Yes, I might have taken a few pictures of her, but I never raped her. I'm out of here. You'll never be able to prove any of this. I have witnesses who will stand up for me."

"Or turn evidence against you to save their own skin. They're coming in next."

Josh glared at Kristina. "Just remember, I might have photos of you everyone will want to see." David Swafford yelled for him to stop, but Josh slammed the door behind him.

Shawn spoke loudly. "Josh just ran out." He received some questionable looks at his words.

Kristina looked like she was in shock. "He drugged me."

The attorney turned to her. "There's no evidence which will hold up in court, Kristina."

Shawn stood and revealed a wireless microphone. "He won't get far, the police are waiting for him outside."

David stood, shoving his chair behind him. "I think we have seen and heard enough. Shawn, you might want to think about finding another job."

Lawson fired back. "In my opinion I think he might be looking at a bonus and whatever else the hell he wants."

"I guess this all depends on what happens to Brent's shares in the company, doesn't it?"

Kelly stretched out her hands to quiet the room. "That will be soon enough, unless the will is blocked by someone. I heard from Brent's attorney who wrote his will today." She turned to Shawn. "He requested you and I both be present this afternoon for a reading."

Shawn watched the people around him pass him looks of varying interest. "Why me?"

"I guess we'll find out. The attorney said it was Brent's wish to have this read immediately upon his death."

"Okay, maybe he'll leave us a clue as to why?" He turned to Lawson. "I'm sure I'll have to visit the police station soon also. You might want to keep Kristina with you until I get all of this taken care of."

Kristina moved forward. "No way, I want to be part of this and hear the truth. I'm not being dumped off." She reached for Shawn's hand.

"They may want a statement at the police department, but I don't think you'll be allowed in the reading of the will."

"I can wait on you here. I'm sure that will not take long, will it?"

Kelly spoke next. "I don't think so. I'll assume he donated most of his assets to charity."

"Good, I'll stay here and wait on you, Shawn."

Shawn's phone rang. "We cannot find Josh. He must be hiding in the building somewhere. We're coming in."

"Wait and I'll join you." He turned to the group. "Josh is hiding in the building somewhere."

The attorney glared at everyone. "I need to go to the entrance and see what I can do to stop this." He rushed out of the room.

"I need to work with my men to do a search of the building. I don't think he's armed or dangerous, just scared."

"Still the same, I think we need to have you with us. I can't wait to hear what the police find out from him." Lawson started biting his lip as he returned to his seat. "I need to find my wife before she hears the breaking news; she'll go berserk."

"I'll call to have one of the drivers take you." Shawn raised his phone.

"Thanks, I know you'll have your hands full here."

"Yes, we'll walk you downstairs, if you wish."

Kelly studied them without saying much. Her mind appeared to be a mile away. "I need to get ready for the meeting this afternoon. It starts at two, Shawn."

"I'll be there."

###

Kristina forced the rage to settle. *Is that what this was, a silly frank to get me naked and photographed? Who are they fooling?* She was pregnant. Someone had their way with her, but who? And importantly, who had the photographs?

With so many questions flooding her mind and no answers, she walked with Shawn and her dad to the elevator. She assumed they would catch Josh soon and make him talk.

As they reached the main floor, Shawn motioned to them to take a side hallway to a place they often used to escape the entrance with possible reporters and the paparazzi. A small entrance from a side street entered a secured entrance used for deliveries and for the company limo. As they walked past one uniformed officer on the way who acknowledged Shawn's security badge, he said, "I need to get a board member out of the building."

"Be careful. We still don't know where Josh is."

"I'll be back to help you find Josh after I get Lawson to the car."

Walking toward the limo, Kristina squeezed Shawn's hand for a moment before asking, "Is it okay if I have a word or two with dad before he leaves?

"Sure, I need to talk to the officer inside for a minute to plan how we're going to hunt for Josh in the building. I'll be inside if you need me."

While the driver held the door open, Kristina gave her father a hug. "I know you and mom may be having a hard time understanding why I want to have this baby, but it's for me to decide this time. This is the first time I've ever had full control of my life, and the possibility of having someone depending on me."

"Your mother and I only have your best interest at heart. You know the only concern we really have is not knowing who the father is. Right now, it could be anyone."

"The doctor told me it was healthy, and should have no known genetic defects. I guess we can thank modern medicine for that. I want to think about something else also."

"Why, what is it?"

"I have lived with you and mom all of life, and it might be time for me to get a place on my own now. This is something I've been thinking about the last few days, since I haven't been home."

"I understand how you feel, but with a baby on the way and no one to be with you to take care of you, it might not be a good idea."

"I have Shawn, and I can hire some people to cook, or . . . I can learn myself."

"Are you planning on moving in permanently with Shawn? I don't think he'll ever be able to support you and give you what you need. He's a nice guy and all, but still, he's just a guard."

"I know, but he had plans, and I don't mind helping him."

"We need to talk, all of us. I don't want him to be using you as his way to make it. That part I don't like. Let me ask you this. You know Shawn's showing you a lot of attention now, which is his job. What do you think he'll do after this problem is behind us? Do you really think he'll want to be a father to your baby?"

"I haven't thought about it in that way, but I kind of hope he would like to be a father. But first I would want to know he would like to be a husband, don't you think. Plus, dad, I think you're rushing things. We haven't known each other too long."

Her father leaned over closer to her. "I've seen the side glance between you two, and the way you hold hands. I can see the signals of love, maybe even much better than you can. As a father, I hope you understand I have reservations."

Kristina knew they had done much more than holding hands. Her father would be shocked to know how many times they had made love. "We'll talk more after this is over. Tell mom I love her."

"I will." He entered the limo as the driver shut the door. She waited until the garage door opened and the limo exited before turning to go inside. Suddenly, a movement caught her eye. A guy was running for the exit—Josh.

"Josh, stop!" Kristina ran after Josh as he raced to the garage door and outside. With no time to spare, she ran under the closing door, with him turning to face her.

He raised a finger as to make a point. "I didn't rape you!"

"Really, someone did. You did drug me, didn't you?"

"It was only supposed to be a prank. You're always so snotty and flirty, but play everyone for a fool. I thought by having photos of you I could take you down a notch. I didn't plan on showing them to anyone but you later."

"You're a sick bastard. I want those photos."

"I don't have them. They have been erased."

"I don't believe you. What did you do to me?"

"I stripped you and took photos of you nude, but that is all. I got scared when I heard someone else coming down the hall and left. I'm not a rapist."

"So, you left me stripped and available to whoever wanted me. You bastard!"

"I didn't think anyone would bother you on the yacht. I was going to see Brent yesterday. I think he might know something, but the old man shot himself first."

"You're going to jail."

"The only way I can be convicted of rape is by you proving you were raped on the yacht. I don't think you can do that. On the photos, it's still your word against mine."

Kristina heard the garage door opening again behind her, with a voice yelling her name. It had to be Shawn.

Josh's eyes widened. "Save us all some embarrassment, have an abortion and walk away from this." He backed away and started running as Shawn ran toward them

Josh glanced over his shoulder as he raced across the street, narrowly missing one car. However, he didn't avoid the next, as the cab hit the brakes too late and knocked him forward before rolling over him. The smoke from the tires bellowed behind the cab as she heard the sound of the screeching tires and people on the street screaming.

She backed into the wall as Shawn raced toward him. Josh had to be hurt bad, maybe killed. Her world faded as the traffic came to a halt on all lanes. She placed one foot in front of another as she inched forward. Rounding one car, she obtained a better look. Shawn was beside him, but the blood covering the pavement behind Josh's head told her what she had feared most.

Chapter 21

Kristina held onto Shawn's arm as she answered one question after another at the police station. Josh had been pronounced dead on the scene. With Shawn's testimony, the cab driver had been cleared on any charges, but visibly shaken as he spoke in broken Russian to Shawn his thank you for helping him to clear his name.

Since Josh died in the accident, there could be no trail to give final closure to her claims of being raped. His DNA had already cleared him of any crime, and any knowledge he had on who it was died with him.

Her dad and an attorney rushed in. "We got here as quick as we could. I heard what happened."

The attorney spoke with the investigating officer. "I'm Ken Foster, the Sutherland family attorney. Is Kristina under any investigation for anything?"

"No, we simply want to gather facts on the accident."

"Since you're asking my client questions, I assume you don't mind if I sit in?"

"Not at all, but we have all I think we need. I have summarized what Shawn and Kristina have told me. I will need them to read it and sign it for me."

Ken looked at Shawn. "Do you have an attorney?"

As Shawn stared to respond a voice behind them spoke. "He does now."

They turned to see Kelly smiling at them. "When you missed the meeting this afternoon I went looking for you. The estate attorney will not read the will until you're present. The meeting has been reset for tomorrow morning."

Shawn rubbed his forehead. "I didn't think about it."

"It's okay. I heard about what happened. You would think someone would have called the company attorney to handle this. Here, let me look at the statement before you sign it."

As the attorneys read the statements, Kristina studied Shawn's eyes. She knew he had much more going on inside his head than he wanted others to know. He had two people killed in front of him the last two days.

Kristina heard more commotions behind her. Her mother had arrived and she was intent on making a scene. She glanced over at Shawn. "What can I say, she's my mom."

Kristina watched Shawn grin for the first time since the accident. "It's good to have someone care about you."

There was no policeman or attorney brave enough to stand between Barbara Sutherland and her daughter. "Baby, I heard what happened. Are you okay?" Barbara frowned at Lawson and Ken.

Ken simply returned to reading the statement as Lawson spoke. "We're almost done. We have to give a statement of what we saw."

Barbara turned to Shawn. "I understand you have been seeing my daughter a lot lately also. We need to talk privately later."

Kelly smiled. "I see nothing wrong with this from a legal standpoint. Still, you need to read this before signing." She handed the paper on to Shawn.

Ken pointed to some of the language. "The conversation with Josh will be hard to prove, and could be used for a libel case, but seeing how he's dead now and unable to do so, I think we're okay."

Kelly arched a brow. "Maybe I look at that?" Ken glanced at Lawson for approval which he gave a yes nod. After reading the statement, Kelly turned toward Kristina. "So, Josh admitted to you that he drugged you?"

"Yes, but he claimed he didn't rape me. I think he knew who, but now we'll never know what he knew. He left me naked and went on his way, leaving me to some other vulture on the boat."

Kelly paused as she looked around. "With several deaths already, I think we need to close this before others get hurt. I know this is hard to take for Kristina, but enough is enough. Kristina, I'm so sorry about all of this. You're like a daughter to me also. I've watched you grow up here."

Kristina watched tears form in her eyes. "Shawn, I have many things to do, but look forward to seeing you on time tomorrow at the reading of the will."

Barbara straightened her back. "Why is Shawn going to be there?"

Kelly stood to leave. "Brent asked him to be at the reading of his will. I'm the only other person he wanted present at the reading. You'll have to ask Shawn after tomorrow morning."

With an indignant look designed to be more show than anything else, Barbara turned to Kristina. "This has been a lot of stress on you. I need you to see my analyst to make sure this doesn't produce any permanent scars on you."

"Mom, I'm so screwed up now, I don't need some shrink really doing a number on me."

"Well . . ."

"Mom, please."

"Okay, we'll talk about it when we get you home."

Kristina turned to her dad. "I don't think I'm going back. I want to start looking for my own place now."

Barbara turned to Shawn. "I guess we have you to thank for this. What have you been placing in my daughter's head?"

Shawn remained silent as Kristina faced her mother. "Shawn has done nothing but allow me to be me. I know you don't like Shawn because he doesn't fit what you think I should be looking for in a man, but he's more man than guys like Josh who you would love to see me with."

Kristina words hit home, as her mother backed away. "We'll talk more later. This isn't the place. So, where are you going now?"

Kristina turned to Shawn. "I'm going with him, if he'll have me." She knew she placed him on the spot, but she hoped he would help her stand her ground.

She watched Shawn turn to her father. "With your permission, sir?"

Lawson turned to Barbara. "I can think of no one who has Kristina best interest at heart more than Shawn. While I don't totally approve of the arrangement, I do approve of Kristina becoming a woman and making her own decisions."

Barbara's mouth dropped. The rest of the people around acted like they were not there as a bomb shell had exploded. Kristina felt extremely proud of her dad and Shawn in the way they had handled it. Now, would her mother come around later?

Chapter 22

Lucy greeted them as they entered Shawn's flat, constantly going back and forth between them. With the smell of the Chinese takeout filled her nostrils, and in spite of being exhausted and mentally spent, she felt hungry. The place might not look like many Fifth Avenue places she knew, but it looked like all of the home she needed right now. And . . . it had Shawn.

"I hope you don't mind me doing that back at the station. I want to be honest with you Shawn. My life's a mess, and I don't know what to do about the baby. It'll be hard to raise a child on my own."

"You've had a long day, and a trying one at that. Tonight, you need to rest."

"I'm not the only one. This has to be hard on you also. I don't know how you do it with no one to call family. You're so independent. I feel like I know you at times, but at others you seem so distant."

"I've never had anyone I could trust before, and I learned to keep to myself."

"You can trust me. I trust you. I want to know you better, if you'll let me."

"Kristina, I trust you, but like you, I don't know what my future holds. With Brent gone from the company, I've no idea what will happen to me. I know Josh's dad will do everything he can to have me fired. I can also see your mother adding to this."

"I've complicated your life, haven't I?"

Shawn smiled for a second. "Yes, but in a good

way. I've enjoyed you being with me. I never thought I would have a beautiful woman seeing where I live."

"Do you really think I'm beautiful?"

"Yes."

"I see, but not very smart."

"Kristina, I think you're much smarter than you allow people to understand."

"So, where do we go from here?"

Shawn pointed to the table and grinned. "How about over there where we can eat."

"Men, I think I'll never figure them out."

"And you've never heard that the way to a man's heart is through his stomach."

"If that's the case, I'm in big trouble."

"Not necessarily, building a relationship is a growing process, a learning process. If you know all of the answers up front, it takes all of the fun out of it."

"So, the question is, do you want me to learn how to cook, and will you be patient with me as I learn?"

"I think we both know I'm a patient man. The question for you is this. Are you patient for me to discover what I want to do with my life?"

"They say a relationship is a lesson in give and take." Kristina reached for the bottle of sake. "And, this they say is a truth serum."

"I've never lied to you."

"I certainly hope so, but I want more. I want to break down the wall around you, and discover who you really are."

"Are you sure you'll like what you find?"

"That depends if you'll allow your heart to stay open."

"My heart?"

"Yes. If you haven't hardened it beyond repair or locked it away, I might have a chance to steal it. But . . . what I would love better is you being able to offer it on your own."

"To me it sounds like you're talking about love. Which is . . . a commitment."

"It may be early, but I would love to know the chance does exist, wouldn't you?"

"That would be nice, but let us face it. I'm not in the league of guys your family would approve of. I could never measure up to what they would expect."

Kristina pressed a finger to his mouth to hush him. "The only person you have to measure up to is me. It's just that I'm having strong feelings for you, and I want to know you're having the same."

"I think you know that."

"Well, hearing it does make a difference to most women."

"Okay, yes I care about you very much. And . . . I hope it will continue to grow."

"So do I." Tonight she would make love to him and make it impossible for him to not fall in love with her and to also tell her so. She wanted him to say those magical words "I love you" first. With no intention of taking no for an answer, she plotted her moves. "Do you mind if I change before we eat?"

"I understand. I think I'll get out of the company uniform and into some jeans myself." He walked to his exposed closet where he kept his clothes as he slipped off his tie, a slim black design matching his fitted black shirt. While not shy about his body, he did turn away from her to place the shirt in his bag where he stored his laundry. While his back muscles displayed the hours of work he dedicated to the gym, the light created a certain glow to his skin, adding a raw sexual energy.

She would have loved for him to watch her strip as much as she enjoyed his show. "I don't know how to thank you for allowing me to use your shirts." Yes, she intended the comment to attract his attention. It worked as he turned, showcasing his abs. Oh damn, he looked good.

"I'm glad to be of service. They look much better on you than they do on me."

Realizing she had not started undressing, Kristina kicked her shoes off and quickly worked on buttons. As he stared directly at her, she loved the attention. While remembering all of the times she had hunted for sexy lingerie, she wore some of the least flattering now. "I promise later to show what I love to wear. I think you'll enjoy it."

Shawn smiled, revealing his white teeth. Yes, she had his interest, so she now needed to work it. She practically ripped off the remaining clothes to where she only had the bra and panties to go. "Do you really think I'm beautiful?"

He dropped his pants as her heart fluttered. She could not have expected any better of an answer. However, instead of dropping his boxers, he leaned over and picked up his pair of jeans. "I think we both know the answer to that question."

Yes, he had told her on many occasions, but it was always in a matter of fact tone. In fact, she never remembered him telling her she looked beautiful with a passion. He had the unique ability to admire beauty and life without touching it. How was she going to get through this wall?

She glanced at the shirt on the side of the bed. Should she remove the last of her clothes, or wait until later? No, she wanted to be ready for him whenever his hormones kicked in. She dropped her panties and then her bra, but he only smiled and didn't walk toward her. His control frustrated her. She was ready to jump his bones right now, right here. Why was he so patient? She closed her eyes, and imagined him making love to her before saying he loved her.

When Kristina opened her eyes, she saw him at the table preparing the Chinese food. She slipped on the shirt and buttoned the buttons at the top, leaving the ones at the bottom open. "It does smell good."

He turned toward her as she touched his shoulder. The feel of warm sexual skin excited her. Perhaps she should confiscate all of his shirts. The definition in his chest muscles mesmerized her as she couldn't take her attention away from them. He had reduced her to a helpless kitten. She pressed forward, and rested her face against his massive muscles as his arms enclosed her in his world. She had no words that would be adequate. She wanted him. "You know . . . you totally own me now."

"Do I?" He ran his hand through her hair. "I'm sure I'm not the only guy with muscles that you can have whenever you wish."

If he thought it was only about sex, he received the wrong message. Sex was simply a way to encourage him to say *I love you*. That was what she really wanted. "I hope you know it's much more than that to me." She raised her focus to his eyes. He wasn't examining her breasts, or any part of her body except her eyes.

She felt him breathe deeply, but maintain his concentrated energy into her soul. "Dance with me." He swayed his body next to hers in a simple step, but one that would bond their bodies together.

"I could enjoy dancing with you every night for the rest of my life." Her head rested on his chest with his smell intoxicating her. She focused on what he must be feeling. He had walls around him, walls she wanted to penetrate. She would give him the best sex he had ever had. There were no limits as to what she would do for him, he had to know that.

"Making love and dancing are the easy parts. I have only had one person in my life that ever cared about me and my future."

Thinking he must be referring to an old girlfriend, she really didn't want to hear the story. "I hope I can change that for you."

"My mom never asked anything from any one. She only wanted me to have a life she never had."

Kristina thought of her parents. She knew they loved her. They had provided her with everything a girl could want. "Parents are like that. This is much like a husband and wife should be, don't you think?"

"I've never had my heart broken. Obviously, I've never allowed it to be subjected to the possibility." He swayed consistently to music she played from her memory.

"How do I get you to trust me?" She realized she might be approaching her goal in the wrong direction. She had always thought great sex would lead to the words *I love you*. Was he trying to tell her the admission of *I love you* led to great sex?"

"I know this sounds funny, but I think by being trustworthy. By being unafraid to say what is on your mind, and . . . to be able to accept me for whom I am. I'm simply a guy with a dream, and a life to share."

"What makes you think any girl would want more than that?"

Shawn glanced around the room. "This is not what you're used to."

"Disappearing inside your world is different. What I want is not so different from what you want. I've lived under the wings of my parents forever, but I want to stretch my own wings now to explore the world. What I really want is someone to share a goal with."

"Okay, then why me?"

"In my life many guys have hit on me. They were all attracted by my family's wealth and position inside the city. I hear the cons all day, every day. I think you're the only man to ever give me compliments, expecting nothing in return."

"I simply admit the truth. The question is—can you handle the truth?"

"I think so, and what do you think the truth is?"

"The truth is—I'm falling in love with you, and I don't know how to handle it."

"If you place your heart in me, I can promise you I'll never allow it to be broken or abused."

"That's one hell of a promise."

She raised her head and stood on her toes to offer a quick kiss on his lips. "It's a promise you have, if you want to accept it."

As he lowered his head to melt his mouth into her lips, his large powerful hands pulled her back snuggly against him. Every muscle inside her body tightened as she dug fingernails into his back. Damn, she would apologize later. She groaned, as he pressed harder.

Shawn slipped his arms under her legs and lifted her off the floor, carrying her as if she was a princess. He kissed the nap of her neck as carried her. Her heart beat even faster as he placed her gently on the side of the bed. She wasted little time in pulling the shirt over her head.

She watched him drop his pants. His erection was obvious even before he dropped his boxers. She stretched her arm to him and touched his dick as he lowered himself on the bed next to her. After turning to face each other, their arms wrapped around each other tightly as her soft breasts pressed into his rock hard chest with the intense feeling of skin on skin quickened her need to have him.

His hand massaged her shoulder before sliding down her side and ending on her rear. His squeeze made her moan again. As she slipped her fingers around his dick, she slightly increased the pressure as she stroked him slowly. While it felt so rock hard, so rigid and ready to take her, it was his eyes focused on her that drove her insane, and walked into her soul to claim all rights to her heart. He had the body she loved, and the mind to take her soul. She increased the intensity of her strokes, since she wanted him inside her and hoped the increased rhythm would drive him as crazy as she was.

She moved slowly on her back and parted her legs. His hand found her crotch and played with her clit, sending her into immediate spasms as she came in record time. Tonight she would not be able to count the times. While she waited on him to mount her, she realized he had not told her the words she wanted. What else could she do?

As he rolled closer to her, she decided on one more trick. With all of the strength she had, she stopped him from mounting her, and lowered her body. She made her intentions obvious.

"You don't have to do that unless you really want to." His words sounded sincere but he barely tried to stop her. Yes, she knew he would love a blow job—most men do.

"I want to. I want to prove to you I'll always make you happy." She pushed lower and adjusted her mouth to his powerful dick, where she offered an immediate lick from the bottom to the top. His shuddering body confirmed his pleasure. She kissed the tip once and heard him moan. The next moment she inhaled him into her mouth. She wished she could accept all of him, but he was too big.

She prepared herself for his ejaculation, and expected him to be loaded. This was the first guy she ever remembered wanting to taste. He had not forced her to do this, she wanted to make him happy.

His voice resonated as an angel approaching her in the best moment in her life. A time she wanted to give, and not worry about being served. "Come up here, please." He pulled her higher as she resisted.

"I can finish you. I know you want it."

"I know you can, but I want to look you in the eyes when I tell you."

"Tell me what?" She moved higher.

He planted a kiss on her lips, as she leveled with him. "I only have one heart to give, and I hope this is the first and last time I have to do this."

Her heart beat faster, as she remained too scared to respond.

"I always thought it would take years for me to fall in love with someone. The last few weeks have been intense. I know what you want from me." He hesitated. Was the wall around him falling? She waited, knowing he had to do this on his own. Forcing him would never do. She knew that now. "I'm . . . not sure what our future holds for us, but all I know is that I have a feeling that is tearing me apart inside. If this is love . . . ." Patience, she needed to control herself. He was almost there. "If this is love than yes, I love you."

Kristina moved closer to his lips and kissed him gently. She wanted him to relax and know she could trust him. "Shawn, I love you to. Do you hear me? I truly love you."

He returned her kiss with the passion she had wanted for days. She reached for his dick again. Sex would be fantastic now. He understood as he rolled on top of her. He adjusted his position to match her as she guided him home. His dick slid in easily, driving her to new levels of pleasure.

She opened her eyes to see him staring at her, still penetrating her soul with each minute. "I love you, Shawn."

"I love you too." He drove harder inside her, and she had to close her eyes as a scream erupted from deep inside her. She hoped to take longer, but how could she? She felt the spasms overtaking her. She couldn't hold it back. She screamed again, as Shawn pumped away with new vigor. Oh god, he was coming, offering her the ultimate climax she had only read about in books. As he lost control and drilled her in rounds and rounds of ecstasy, she felt tears falling down her face. Oh, my god!

Suddenly, he stopped. He had to be totally exhausted. She was. She ran her hands through his hair, and in spite of all of his raw sexual power, he acted like a kitten in her hands now. He asked for trust which she knew she would always give. Since his future was now her future, she had to make it work. "Sleep my love. You have a big day tomorrow."

Chapter 23

Shawn walked through Kelly's office and on to a conference table on the far side, where a gentleman was sitting at the table reading some papers. "We have been waiting on you. Let me introduce you to Mr. Lacky, who wrote the will for Brent."

When Mr. Lacky heard the introduction he stood and walked around the conference table to shake Shawn's hand. Shawn had visions of what might be in the will. Since he was there, he hoped he might finally be given knowledge about his past, and maybe enough money to start his own private agency.

Shawn shook the hand of a man intent on studying him. "I heard you wanted me to attend the reading."

"Yes. I think you'll leave here very happy, but sad at the same time. It's my job to do your grandfather's wishes."

Kelly stumbled on her way to a seat. "What did you say?"

"Shawn had agreed to never mention this to save face for his grandfather, but now that Brent has died, he wanted everyone to know. I think this will become clearer as I read his last words. Shall we begin?"

Kelly began to tremble, as she waited on Mr. Lackey to start reading. While Shawn felt a newfound pride building inside of him, he wondered about what he meant about being sad.

Mr. Lacky placed a recorder on the table. "I hope no one has a problem with this, but it's required."

Kelly and Shawn exchanged nods as he began to read. "Being of sound mind and body I have rewritten my will I hope for the last time. A copy is attached for the courts to process. I wanted to include this letter which Shawn may do with as he sees fit. I have a lot of explaining to do. Knowing what Shawn will be facing, I wanted the head lawyer, Kelly, attending this reading also."

The lawyer cleared his throat and continued, "When my daughter ran off with a drummer for a rock and roll band many years ago, it broke my heart and caused me more anguish than I could handle. I had lost control of the one life I want to keep close to me. I never could recover from it. When the guy she ran off with deserted her and she needed me, I wasn't there for her. I was too embarrassed to take her back, and I worried only about myself and my precious reputation."

Another pause. "When I heard she was pregnant, I thought it served her right, and I definitely wanted nothing to do with her or her illegitimate baby. I'm so sorry Shawn. I know how tough it had to be on you. I always planned on making it right one day, but she died before I could. It took me a while after that to find you, but even then my pride got in the way. You'll never know how proud I am of you for keeping our secret when you came to work here."

As Kelly nervously twitched her fingers on the table, he continued, "I thought about giving my money to charity and letting you make money the way I did, and I think you have all of the qualities needed to do so. However, I have given charities money for a long time, and it's time to do something for my family.

With the exception of a separate trust of five million that I have directed my attorney to set up, I want all the remaining assets given to you. I hope you manage them well."

Shawn had no clue how much this was, but knew he would be very rich.

After looking over the top of his glasses, the attorney continued to read. "Now, for a confession. I know this will come out eventually. I've done something I'm very much ashamed of. Something I have no excuse for. Something I wish I could erase. On the night of the cruise where we all heavily celebrated a new acquisition, I, like many attendees, enjoyed way too much champagne, and in my case scotch. I tried to clear my head by going outside for fresh air, and then downstairs to rest for a minute. I stumbled into one of the cabins to find a naked woman lying on a bed. She woke long enough to give me a hug and acted so sexy."

Shawn knew he was talking about Kristina, as he continued, "I thought she acted this way all of the time and with such a come on I played along with her and never remember how fast it happened, but I soon had sex with her. It wasn't until after we were finished that I knew she was totally out of it. Afraid of what I had done, I left her like she was and never said anything because I thought it would be impossible to get someone pregnant at my age. This sin I will take to my grave, but I hope this confession and money will help some. I never intended to hurt anyone and ask you to forgive this old fool."

The attorney glanced toward the ceiling. "We had a conversation about this, but he didn't give me details of this letter. I only read it the first time yesterday."

Kelly glanced at both of them. "This letter should prove he raped Kristina, especially if his DNA will confirm it. However, since he's dead now, there should be no prosecution. We have to decide how much we want to disclose to the public."

Shawn looked at both. "Kristina deserves to know the truth. This might make a big difference in her deciding if she wants to keep the baby or not."

Lacey turned toward Kelly. "This will make Shawn the main stockholder in the company."

Kelly turned to Shawn. "I never knew this. He never shared it with me. This must have been hard on you to work here, and his death must be devastating on you. At least we can tie up all of the pieces now."

"Almost everything. We still have his death to consider."

Kelly shut her file as if to ignore him. "I think with this confession it's obvious he had motive to commit suicide."

Shawn turned to Lacey. "How long ago did he change this will?"

"Just a few days ago. He called and told me he wanted it done right away. I don't have the previous copy. He was intent on destroying it. However, I'm sure he had you mentioned in the will."

"I want you think hard. Did he look like a man about to commit suicide?"

"Not really, if he did I would have found him some help. He has been a good client for a long time, and a good friend."

"We all heard he had words with Josh. We need to know what that was about, and if it was something that pushed him over the edge. I still think he didn't pull the trigger."

"Do you think it was Josh?"

"I don't know for sure, but I don't think so for several reasons. He would know there was no way he could get away with it. Since both of you are attorneys, let me ask this question. If Josh had nothing to do with the rape, but only the drugging and photographing he claimed, wouldn't he also be charged with the rape as an accomplice and thus rape, if it was proved she was raped?"

Lacey answered. "There's a strong chance you're right. If Brent was about to cave in and plead guilty to rape, it would increase his chances of being found guilty of rape also. It's an interesting theory."

Shawn glanced around "Can we delay announcing this for a day or two until I check out something?"

Kelly glanced at Lacey for advice. "I'm sure the police will want to know what was in Brent's file. And I'm sure they'll have many questions for you Shawn, since you're the main beneficiary."

Shawn handed Kelly a piece of paper. "Can you give me your cell phone number where I can reach you later?"

"I thought you already had it." She smiled and wrote her number using her left hand, which confirmed what he thought. He needed to see who else used their left hand, and was close to Brent when he died.

"Thanks. I also want to be the first one to tell Kristina. She deserves the truth." Shawn stood and walked over to Lacey. "I want to thank you for everything. I know I'll have many questions."

Mr. Lacey stood and shook Shawn's hand. "I need to conclude the tape we have by saying Brent's will and letter have been read to those he had given me instruction to do so. I'll be recording the will shortly. The personal letter is up to Shawn to do with as he pleases."

Chapter 24

Shawn stopped to buy some champagne as the words sunk in. He was going to be rich, oh shit yes, very rich. Life would change. He felt glad to have a day to prepare for this. At the same time, he knew his days of hiding in the shadows were over; he would now be the one in the spot light.

He had only one person he wanted to tell first. The one thing that had been holding him back from moving forward with her has been money. Sorry, but true. While he wanted to take care of her, he now had a new obstacle caused by the same. He didn't want her to love him because he had money either. There had to be a middle ground somewhere, and he only had tonight to find the answer.

Shawn had watched her coping with her own situation. The truth was being revealed, and one of the final key puzzle pieces would be disclosed to her tonight. He still wondered how she would take the news, especially when she hears it was his grandfather who performed the ghastly deed.

After climbing the last of the stairs, he pushed inside his flat. Kristina was all smiles in seeing him enter. She had changed to the casual side he loved to see in her. She was much more fun to be around when she allowed herself to relax.

"I have some champagne for us tonight, and as I promised, I have some news for us to discuss."

"I hoped you would be back soon. I've missed

you." She walked over to him and gave him a big kiss directly on his lips with a passion he loved. She stared at the champagne. "You still haven't explained why you wanted champagne."

"To be honest, today has been a mixed bag. I think your father kind of likes me. What do you think?"

"My dad wants me to be happy. He has his ways. Yes, I think he would love for me to marry a rich young businessman, much like he was at our age, but I think he'll come around to seeing us happy. Now, mom it'll take a while longer for her, but she will in time."

"I like your dad. He's very smart and capable of running the company."

"He has always wanted to be president, but only has a small share of the stock. Now, that Brent has died I know he's anxious as to who the new major stockholder will be and how it will affect him."

"I don't think he has anything to worry about."

"That's right. You went to the reading of the will today. Do you have any news you want to disclose on who that might be?"

"I might, but first I have some news for you I think you need to hear. I know more of the story of what happened to you that night on the cruise."

Kristina lost her smile. "I know Josh drugged me. What else have you learned?"

"I think it would be best to let you read a letter I received today. I know this will be hard on you, and I'm here for you. I have, however, cut it into two parts. I'll show you the first part last. I hope you'll trust me on this."

He handed the part of the letter where Brent

admitted having sex with Kristina and waited on her to read. Her face turned harsh. "No, I can't believe this."

"Only I and Kelly have this information. It's not part of the will, and no one will know unless you want them to. The decision was left up to me, and I'm leaving it up to you."

"How old is Brent, like, seventy five, right?"

"I think that will be close. I know you must hate him, but he's not here anymore."

"So, that is why he committed suicide?"

Shawn presented some photos he had with him. "I'm not so sure, I have something else I want you to see later. There's one more reason I wanted to talk to you tonight, and the reason for the champagne. But first, I have one question for you. I hoped to ask this later, but I feel like I need to ask it now, for both of us."

Looking complex, Kristina leaned sideways against the couch. "What is it?"

"We've known each other for only a very short time, but a lot has happened to us. If I'm presumptuous on this please let me know." Shawn swallowed hard, as he studied her face.

"I understand what you're saying. I never thought this would be happening to me. If you think I've taken advantage of you because you work for my dad, I'm sorry. I've enjoyed the time we've spent together. I heard Josh's dad wants you fired from the company. I'm willing to work with you, and start from scratch if that's what it takes to stay with you."

Encouraged by the words he heard, Shawn decided to run with them. "What if starting over meant leaving New York, and exploring the world out there?"

"Since I have no one in New York besides my parents, who often are overbearing, it could be an option. All I know now is . . . I want to be with you. I want you to open up to me and tell me more about you. I want to find a way inside your heart and soul. That's what will make me happy."

"So, as they say in the marriage vows so often: are you ready for a better or worst commitment?"

"For me to consider a partner for life, I think it would have to be that way. You know . . . my dad might forsake me and never give me a dime."

"If I understand you correctly you can accept me as I am, and with the understanding I might never have anything material to really give you."

"Yes, I can honestly say that."

"And when I later make my mark and become wealthy, will you still want to find a place like this to hide away and keep what we have?"

"I think staying out of the spotlight would be great."

"Good." He leaned over and kissed her lips, melting into her deeper than he had in a long time. "I think you need to read the first part of the letter my grandfather left me."

"Grandfather?"

Chapter 25

Kristina finished the letter. "He sounded sincere, but it does make me sound like a slut. I'm not sure I want anyone to read this." She handed the letter back to Shawn.

"I didn't think you would, but hoped it might add some closure for you. Your baby would be well taken care of with the foundation he has planned."

"Yes, I can see that, but money hasn't been on my mind. Knowing who the father is has been."

"And now that you know?"

"Well, at least it's not some ugly person with a deep dark secret I would always be scared of." She smiled, as she realized one fact. "Have you considered the fact this baby would be like an aunt, or uncle, or something to you?"

"The thought has occurred to me. We would share some genes."

"This is going to make the decision much more complicated. Since you share some kinship . . . ."

"I see. Do you think I would make a good father figure?"

"It's up to you if you want to apply for the job or not."

Shawn poured her another glass of champagne. "I always assumed I would be a father at some time. All of this has happened fast for both of us."

"You know I never asked for any of this, but in a way it has opened my eyes to a whole new world. I do know one thing for sure that I don't mind telling you. I don't want to lose you. I want to spend time with you. I want to be part of your life if you'll let me and now . . . ." She rubbed her stomach. "I hope you want to be a part of mine and this."

She watched him close his eyes while she patiently waited on him to complete his thoughts. "We have many things to work out. It won't be easy, but I can tell you I have never wanted to be with anyone more than you. I think you can count on me always being there for you."

"I also understand how many details have to work out. And, oh my god, Dad's going to totally flip out when he hears you're going to be his new boss."

She watched Shawn stare at the ceiling. "I know nothing about running a company this size. I don't have the education or the experience to do so."

"I'm sure that will come in time."

"Maybe so, but until later I think your dad's the best one to take the company forward. You know, just because I own the stock, it doesn't mean I have to run the company."

"You would make my dad the happiest man in the world if you promoted him to the CEO of the company."

"In turn, he would make me happy if he accepted the position." Kristina raised the glass again. "Perhaps we should have invited him here."

Shawn laughed the way she loved to hear him when he let his guard down. "I hardly think he would approve of this place, but a party is in order, especially if I'm going to ask him one important question."

Kristina's heart fluttered. She would love to see

Shawn and her dad become good friends. Her mother might be another story, but his sudden wealth would change her tone quickly. Sad but true, but she also knew Shawn may have plans of not letting anyone know he had inherited such wealth. It would be like him.

He leaned forward. "If I'm to propose to you, I want to pick the time and place. Is that a problem?"

"No, not at all. As long as you don't take forever." She added a giggle, as the excitement of a surprise played in her mind. She glanced at the small package he had on the side table. "You said you have photos you wanted me to see."

"Yes, and this is serious. I didn't notice this earlier, but wanted you to see something."

She examined a few photos of her walking around the celebration cruise. She had seen these several times before. He showed her a few new ones where she walked on the main cabin. She looked dazed. "What are these?"

"These are a few taken the next morning, as you left the yacht. They were taken by a security camera we use to watch the yacht while it's docked."

"I see. What is it you want me to notice?"

"Here look closer now." He handed her a magnifying lens.

She raised the lens and winked. "Now I really feel like a detective."

"Take a look at your clothes closer. Especially your scarf."

Her mind suddenly captured the difference; small but significant. "It's tied differently. One is a right handed tie, and the other is a left handed tie."

"Do you always tie it the same way?"

"Yes, only left handed people tie it that way. I never do. This proves someone else dressed me some time during the night." She turned to Brent's letter. "He said he left me nude. So, who dressed me? When I woke I was fully dressed."

"A left handed person. When I saw my grandfather shot and lying on his desk, the gun shot came from the left side of his head and the gun was in his left hand. He has never been left handed."

"Do you think the two facts are related?"

"Yes, but why, I don't know yet. I think I know someone that does. The problem is . . . she may be involved. You have to trust me on this hunch."

"Shawn since I want to spend my life with you, of course I trust you." She squirmed. "But damn it, this is my life too, and you said she; who is it?"

Chapter 26

Shawn held Kristina's hand as they walked into Kelly's office. She looked at them, but with no emotions showing. "You make a good lucking couple."

"Thanks. We have a long ways to go, but I think we'll make it." Shawn walked toward the conference table "I appreciate you giving me a day to consider some things before we release the disclosures in the will."

"As the attorney mentioned when he read the will, the private letter Brent wrote to you will not be made public unless you decide to do so."

"I'm sure many people will want to know why he willed his estate to me and established a special fund for Kristina."

"Yes, but they'll have to live with it. What have you decided to do?"

Shawn pulled out a chair for Kristina, who remained quiet, as he hoped she would. "I'm sure Kristina will have her say in a minute, but I still have some unanswered questions."

"Such as?"

"I don't think either Josh or Brent were behind the attacks on Kristina, or asking her to have an abortion."

"Really!"

"I also don't believe my grandfather committed suicide."

"Why is that?"

"The gun was in his left hand, and we all know he's not left handed. There's something else I want to show you." He tossed her some photos. "Do you see something strange about the scarf Kristina is wearing? As opposed to the way she tied it the night before."

"And your point is?"

"With the note from my grandfather saying he left her nude, someone else must have dressed her. That person was left handed." Shawn squared his eyes at Kelly. "You're left handed, aren't you?"

"I think you're using a lot of circumstantial evidence to build a case, if you think I had anything to do with this."

"I think after you shot my grandfather, you moved to the side of the room, and waited until Josh entered before you slid in behind him, maybe hoping he would take the rap for your deed."

"You know, proving this would be impossible."

"I'm not so sure, but I still want to know why? What was in it for you?"

"For me? Nothing. I attempted to do a good deed, and ended up screwing up everything. I found Kristina in the cabin later, she was totally naked, and I assumed the worst had happened. I could also tell you were totally out of it. I cleaned you up, and dressed you, hoping it would never be discovered. And it would have remained hidden, that is, if you hadn't become pregnant. No one would've ever known."

Kristina broke her silence. "You knew I had been raped, and you said nothing."

"I saw Brent walking the hallway and suspected he might be the one, but at his age I thought it would be impossible for him to make you pregnant."

"But why the silence later, and why the threats to push me into having an abortion?"

"If it could ever be proved you were raped later, I

could be held accountable as an accomplice."

Shawn understood everything now. Well almost. "But why did you kill Brent?"

"It was an accident. It wasn't supposed to happen. He was going to expose everything. I pulled the gun away from him. Yes, he planned to call the police to confess. When I attempted to take the gun from him, it went off. I had to act fast. There's one thing I didn't tell you. I had a crush on your grandfather for all of my life. I couldn't stand to see him throw it away at the end of it, and I wanted his life to be remembered for the good he did."

Shawn looked at Kristina. "We have answers. Now, can we live with them?" Kelly's right, it'll be impossible to prove any of this. I hope she can live with what she did."

Kristina held Shawn's hand as they walked out of the building and toward his car. "This place will never be the same."

"You're right, it will be better. I need to let your dad know what he has to look forward to, and he can decide if he wants to fire her or not. I'll put complete control in his hands. I'll certainly have mine full."

Kristina squeezed his hand harder. "I remember you saying you needed to ask my dad another question . also."

"I've been thinking of something. We both want to see what the world looks like outside New York. Are you interested in a road trip?"

"Like where?"

"I'm thinking Las Vegas."

"What could we do in Las Vegas?"

"I did promise you a surprise, and if I ask your dad now he might want to make plans for a large wedding, and that's not the way I think we need to start things off."

"Now what makes you think I'll marry a guy like you?"

"Because you love me."

"Are you sure about that?"

"Yes."

"And why is that?"

"Because I'm in love with you and never do anything halfway."

Kristina hugged him, and kissed his lips, as she allowed all anguish from the ordeal over the last few weeks to disappear. "I want to start over with you also, and yes, I love you, Shawn."

THE END

www.ingramcontent.com/pod-product-compliance
Lightning Source LLC
Chambersburg PA
CBHW070311190726
48291CB00012B/1074